T0142538

Cricket Maiden

*Romance, Match-Fixing, Murder mystrey,
T20 Matches, and a Magic Cricket Bat.....*

ALGENES EDMUND DANTES

Order this book online at www.trafford.com
or email orders@trafford.com

Most Trafford titles are also available at major online book retailers.

Second edition in January 2013 by Algenes Aranha

Address:
7/269 Riverside Boulevard
Douglas 4814
Townsville
Queensland
Australia

E-mail: Algenes.Edmund@gmail.com
Website: www.cricketmaidennovel.com

Cover design: Nicole Jacobs

Printed in the United States of America.

ISBN: 978-1-4669-7917-8 (sc)
ISBN: 978-1-4669-7916-1 (hc)
ISBN: 978-1-4669-7918-5 (e)

Library of Congress Control Number: 2013901727

Trafford rev. 01/28/2013

 www.trafford.com

North America & international
toll-free: 1 888 232 4444 (USA & Canada)
phone: 250 383 6864 ♦ fax: 812 355 4082

Contents

Chapter 1

India, in 1810

It was a hot Indian summer afternoon in Bangalore. The match between the East India Company XI and the Deccan XI was at the boil.

It was the tea interval on the fifth and final evening between the two sides. The annual Colonial Championship finals trophy was at stake.

The spectators at the Sir Russell Rawlinson Stadium could scarcely believe the climax that this year's championship final had reached. The visiting East India Company XI needed sixteen runs more to win, in a maximum of thirty overs between the tea interval and the close of play. Although a perfectly manageable chase, they had only two wickets in hand, which their opponents, Deccan XI, were pursuing to ensure their win.

The stadium was dusty, dry, with a sparse grassing in the outfield. The wickets were matted as they were in the days of old. The boundary line for the playing field was delineated by a thick rope. The majority of the supporters were British colonial public servants and their families, with a generous mix of the Indian elite in attendance.

They had watched the game for the last five days, with watchful expectations. Not out and batting with growing confidence was the youthful twenty-four-year-old Hughie Dawson, the last recognized batsman from the East India Company XI. Batting on eighty-four runs, their hopes of victory largely rested upon his young shoulders, sharp mind, quick reflexes, and good hand-eye coordination with the bat. He was batting in the company of Lord Frederick Clarkson, the leading bowler for the East India Company XI, who batted at number 10. Slated at number 11 was the last man, Harold Wellington.

The players wore white clothing, a standard requirement for all cricket matches and prior to the arrival of colored clothing in the 1970s. The absence of diving catches and saves by fielders in that era meant that the clothing remained unblemished by the dusty fields. The old-fashioned black-colored batting gloves and pads, the black belts, the black formal shoes that were in that era before trainers were all on display for the even thirty thousand spectators to witness.

The main pavilion, built of brick and stone and painted white, had canopies and round tea tables with chairs for the elite. The stewards had trays of wine and cheese and were as industrious as bumblebees in their red outfits.

The elite, seated in the main pavilion, mainly consisted of the British colonial representatives, the British military, and rulers of Indian princely states, their wives and families. The public, seated on the cemented, tiered insteps that served as seats, were boisterous in admiration of this noblest of sports unfolding before them. The umpires on the field were gregarious elderly men with long gray beards and white physician's lab coats.

A hawker within the stadium was selling *bhel puri*, *pani puri*, and cut coconut to the spectators. The Indian public wore outfits that were wholly representative of every culture that inhabited India. The ladies adorned saris and *salwar kameezes* of every hue, and the bangles, *bindis*, and earrings only served to complete the plethora of color, which made the stadium more picturesque. The men wore a combination of standard British shirts and pants, along with *khadi dhotis* and turbans.

The overall atmosphere of the scents, the colors, the noise, superimposed on the gaudy Indian summer day, made the scene archetypical of cricket in the nineteenth century.

The teams' dressing rooms would normally be subdued and tension filled in such circumstances. But not on this occasion, as this had everything to do with match fixing.

The bookmakers were led by Brian Cashman. He was a popular bookmaker in Britain, placing bets on horses and grayhounds, and had discovered the lucrative potential of match fixing in cricket in double-wicket championships. He was now at the right place at the right time to really make an impact and influence the result of a major first-class cricket championship final.

Cashman, who was bald with gray hair on the back of his head, walking with a characteristic limp favoring his right foot, and a sleazy face, approached Lord Clarkson and Harold Wellington and boldly declared, "I wish to make a proposal to ye honorable gentlemen, a promise of a sizable sum of money to throw away this match." Cashman wasn't ashamed of his declaration; he didn't need to be. It was, after all, business as usual for him in an era of match fixing.

The cricket world was plagued by match fixing in the nineteenth century. This sin of match fixing and bookmakers offering large sums of money to players to underperform, and hence alter the course of a match, was a widespread practice. It was only with the intervention of the Marylebone Cricket Club, which had banned bookmakers in cricket since the 1820s, that cricket had a chance to flourish without match fixing.

Cashman had bribed Lord Clarkson before—notably in club cricket fixtures in England. The pittance of a salary made from playing club matches and the vast sums offered by bookies was primarily the reason match fixing flourished as well as it did.

Clarkson was approaching the age of forty when fast bowlers started to slow down.

Wellington was an amateur who primarily worked as an accountant in Calcutta and wasn't really a penetrating wicket-taking bowler; he was mainly a container of runs, with his tight line and lengths when bowling off spin. In other words, fairly dispensable for the next season if a better and a more dynamic younger bowler came along. With their cricket-playing careers almost inevitably coming to an end soon, they had no difficulty in deciding what to do with Cashman's match-fixing proposal.

Cashman had two brown envelopes under his arm, which he handed over to Lord Clarkson and Wellington. "That's fifty thousand pounds for each of you two to dismiss yourself at the earliest possible opportunity. The match will end with a narrow victory for the home team. I have accumulated a mammoth sum of money from the honorable ladies and gentlemen of the audience who have placed their bets largely in favor of the home team being able to take the last two wickets of the visitors before the remaining sixteen runs are scored, to ensure a victory. If the result goes otherwise, I stand to lose out on a lot of money."

"You need not worry about that, Mr. Cashman," said Lord Clarkson, his eyes gleaming, head woozy, and adrenaline pumping through his belly at his newly acquired wealth. "I will ensure that the match ends in their victory."

"But there's this Dawson problem," continued Lord Clarkson. "He comes from a cricketing family. His father served in the Crimean War and then later on turned into a cricket administrator and curator of the East India Company's shipping department. He passed away a few years ago. Their family estate is at a hill station in Darjeeling, in the north of India. He plays very good strokes off both his front and back foot, on both sides of the wicket. He is still batting."

"Perhaps you could get him to run on a midfield and facilitate a run out. I could arrange that with the Deccan XI players," said Cashman.

All this was within Vijay's earshot. The young friend of Hugh Dawson, Vijay, at the age of fourteen, was full of wonder for cricket and its cricketers. He ran to the military families' stand to tell his friend Hughie Dawson about this plot he had just overheard.

At the members' stand was Hughie with his fiancée, the gorgeous twenty-year-old Andalusia Battersby. "Hugh, they are trying to get you out. You must do something." Hughie was putting his thigh pads on, preparing to go out to bat, when he froze in silence at those words. What despicable individuals would want to throw a match away at such a crucial stage in the final session of the annual finals?

Hugh approached his long-time mentor, a friend of his late father and batting coach, Lord Gregory, who was dressed in his military uniform and seated under a canopy at the main pavilion, sipping a cup of English Breakfast tea. Upon hearing of this plot, Lord Gregory pondered for a few minutes, his thick eyebrows and forehead creased in deep thought, which added to his clean-shaven face a calm and wise demeanor. "Cricket has long suffered from match fixing. All the rotten apples are in one basket now—the match fixers and the bribed players. It's time to set them all straight with one swift stroke. It's time to bring in *Penta*."

"What's *Penta?*" asked a bewildered Hugh.

"Before your father passed away, he told me of the times he survived the war in the Crimea. It was to do with a magical piece of golden rod, about twelve inches long and cylindrical, whose origins are uncertain. But it had the ability to allow bullets to deflect off its bearer. It was primarily used as a survival tool in the trenches. And rather accidentally discovered, and more interestingly, was its ability to attract a cricket ball to reach right in the middle of it, no matter where it gets bowled from, no matter what the swing, and then fly past fielders for runs. He realized the dark, shady people who wanted to get hold of such a bat—and so left it in the hands of the Shepherd's Triad. We, for our part, inserted the rod into a wooden bat, and this has evaded match fixers for years now."

The match was barely a few minutes away from resuming for the fifth and final session. An impatient and emotional Vijay, with a wide-eyed stare, asked in confusion, "The umpires will soon walk out. We start soon. What are we to do?"

Lord Gregory smiled calmly. "I foresaw this moment, when the uncouth would dare to pervert the noble ideals of our sport. I am one of the three members of this Shepherd's Triad. I have the object in question with me." He spread open the left side of his coat to reveal a small wooden bat with a polished copper handle strapped within it.

Hugh exclaimed, "That's not a golden rod!"

"Your eyes deceive you, young Hugh," explained Lord Gregory. "The Penta rod is half the handle of the bat, and the other half is embedded within the meat of the bat. It has been coated brown on the outside. Countless match fixers have been after this bat for years. But the Shepherd's Triad is so secretive that the match fixers have never and will never be able to find it. Now is the time to use it and save the honor of cricket."

"But how do I use it?" asked Dawson.

"Well, just like you would any other ordinary bat. It just has a mind of its own—it connects the ball in the middle of the bat and flies for runs well away from fielders. This will ensure we fight fire with fire and score the remaining sixteen runs to win and foil the match fixers' plans, hopefully, for good."

"And what happens later, after the match is won and it's all over?" Hughie Dawson asked.

"Simple," said Lord Gregory. "We return the bat back to our second representative of the Shepherd's Triad in India— my steward, Errol, who lives at my mansion at the Nandi Hills. It's where your father wished the bat to be kept. Our third contact is in the Caribbean, in Kingston, Jamaica, another friend of your father's. I am the leader and will be voyaging back to England shortly, keeping this secret inside me."

The crowd cheered as the Deccan XI fielders walked out to the field. Lord Clarkson waited impatiently for his batting partner, Hugh Dawson, to join him at the gates. Hugh appeared, carrying a new bat. Clarkson, as watchful as a hawk, noticed this new appendage in the equation to his riches and gasped, "Goodness me, Hughie, my son, what's this you've got out?"

Hugh lied, "It's just a new bat I thought I'd try. May be good enough for me to score the remaining few runs and bring up my century."

"Now, now, young man, don't be so greedy. We tailenders want to score a few runs too, you know," said Lord Clarkson, with a false smile and laugh.

Lord Clarkson turned his head away to meet the eyes of Brian Cashman in the dressing room. The look on his face conveyed the message of impending doom, as he sensed the determination and optimism of his young batting partner intending to score all the remaining sixteen runs needed to win the match.

He turned back in time to see Hugh blowing a kiss to his young fiancée in the crowd.

"What's she to you, Hughie?" an irked Clarkson asked.

"She means the world to me," said Dawson. "She is my equal in the world. She is the source of everything good that has happened to me, my inspiration to wake up each morning. She is the biggest reason I took up cricket again, after the untimely death of my father. She is, in my opinion—"

"Oh, give over, Hughie, you've made your point," interrupted an irritable Clarkson. "Just as long as you score the runs and win us the match. Remember, I'm batting and you will be at the nonstriker's end for the start of the over." With those words, they walked out to the middle.

The first ball was bowled by the Deccan XI medium-pace bowler McCaughey, wide off the off stump, and Lord Clarkson did everything possible to either intentionally nick it to the wicketkeeper or slips fieldsmen—only to miss miserably. He saw Hugh's eyes widen at the bowler's end. "Don't look at me like that, son. I'm old enough to be your father!" screamed back Clarkson.

The second ball, down the leg side, a wide (a legitimate delivery in 1810), was missed by the wicketkeeper, and Clarkson decided to run for the bye in order to not instill suspicion in his batting partner that this match was fixed. Fifteen more runs to win. There were still plenty of overs to go.

Now, Hugh Dawson had strike and took guard. The third ball was bowled short and wide off the off stump, and Hugh punished it for four runs with a ferocious square cut past square leg. Eleven more runs to win. Dawson's score moved onto 88 runs from 84. The spectators clapped and cheered in appreciation of the good shot.

Fourth delivery—dug in short—and Dawson hooked. The bat connected with the ball, and it flew over the midwicket fence for 6 runs. The crowd cheered even more with the 2 shots played that had just yielded 10 runs. Dawson's score moved onto 94 runs, with only 5 more runs needed by the visiting batting team to win the match.

Lord Frederick Clarkson appeared shaken—his well-laid plans to lose his team the match were not going according to the scheme. He turned to the umpire. The umpire winked back and declared, "I have been paid by Cashman as well to give a leg-before-wicket dismissal on flimsy grounds to Dawson, but the ball just never hit his pads all innings."

Fifth delivery. A good one down the corridor of uncertainty, an off-stump line—and swinging in late—well defended by Dawson, off the middle of the bat.

The sixth delivery, again a good length ball was deflected to the on side by Dawson. Seeing the incoming fielder running in from long on to field the ball, Dawson wanted to take a single to move over to the nonstriker's end. He signaled to Clarkson to take a single, but Clarkson pretended to not hear his call and stayed his ground at the nonstriker's end, hoping that Dawson would be run out. The throw from the Deccan fielders missed the stumps at the striker's end, and Dawson safely made it back.

"It must be so hard for my love, playing with a team of prideless losers," said Andalusia. "I want the team to win for his sake but also wish they lose for the sake of his 'teammates.' They don't deserve to win."

"Well," said Lord Gregory, "the game's governing body in London, the Imperial Cricket Council, is very concerned about all this match fixing and is about to put an end to it fairly soon."

The next over was bowled by a spinner, and a desperate Clarkson made room and deliberately stepped outside his crease to allow himself to get stumped—only to see the wicketkeeper miss the ball and for it to roll harmlessly down to the slips. He went for an impossible run on the next ball and hoped he would run himself out, but the throw reached Dawson's end, whose electric running between the wickets made it back to the striker's end in good time.

"How was that possible?" screamed Clarkson. How could such improbable events contrive to prevent him from running out Dawson or himself? The fielders had it so easy! And the target to win was now down to four runs.

Next ball to Dawson. The fielders came in closer; the crowd waited with bated breath. Full toss. Dawson swept; he connected cleanly with the ball, which was a classical off-spinner, six over backward square leg!

With one stroke, Hugh Dawson brought up his century and won his team the match, the series for the 1810 season. This was not what his teammates wanted, for they had been bribed to lose the match. Clarkson, at the other end, could scarcely believe his team's two-wicket victory despite all his attempts to thwart it. He fell onto his knees in exasperation. Hughie had single-handedly scored 100 out of the 140 runs needed to win in the fourth innings. Hugh gave a shriek of joy, punched his fist into the air, and rushed to the pavilion, to the love of his life. He grabbed Andalusia and lifted her off her feet and twirled her around. Vijay danced around the happy couple. Lord Gregory smiled knowingly in the background.

The spectators were delighted with the finish. For them, the visiting team winning the match and the championship was overshadowed by that brilliant century from Hughie Dawson. Cricket had won first blood over the match fixers.

Chapter 2

Dame Andalusia and Hughie Dawson—1810 In Bangalore, Colonial India

The postmatch celebratory events took place at the Sunset Villa that night. The championship trophy was to be handed over to the captain of the East India XI, and all the players were feted. Hughie and Andalusia were having a private walk in the nearby Cubbon Park gardens, leaving the revelers to carry on their celebrations into the night.

Andalusia was dressed in a purple corset and evening gown, and her long brown hair was tied at the back in a bun. She was wearing her favorite Pavlova perfume. Of half-Spanish and half-English ancestry, she had large blue eyes, high cheekbones, luscious lips, and a short athletic body. She loved to see her man, Hughie, play cricket. Hughie was wearing his favorite black tuxedo suit.

Andalusia said, "Oh, Hughie, when will we be able to enjoy our lives together? You have done so well at cricket lately. I long to return to England someday."

Hughie replied, "We'll sail back to England by the end of this year, perhaps. I may begin an education at Cambridge. We'll have a large church wedding someday. We'll then raise our beautiful children and travel the world and conquer the world."

The couple reached a bench in the middle of the park. It was surrounded by red and blue roses, and the large green grass and the last few rays of the setting sun made it the perfect precedent for what was to follow. The flight of the evening birds in the sky was the only movement in the scene of flourishing, rich, colorful botany. Hugh reached into his pocket and brought out a diamond ring.

Andalusia gasped at the size of the large diamond in the center and the two smaller ones beside the main one. Hugh knelt by her side and asked her if she would marry him. Andalusia agreed. Their love had survived the test of time, ever since they first felt those juicy emotions as teenagers growing up in England. Hugh was such a respectful gentleman and had this warrior spirit, as he had shown on the cricket field today.

They shared a warm embrace and a deep, private kiss in the park, only witnessed by the splendor of the gardens, leaves, trees, grass, and flowers that surrounded them. These eternal soul mates felt their heartbeats synchronize, and the power of love in their intimate, romantic embrace was the overall winner. Moments later, a voice was heard, ending their intimacy, calling out, "Hugh, where are you?"

They turned around to see Vijay searching around the park, looking a little lost. "What happens to be the problem, Vijay?" asked Hugh.

"The guests are leaving. Lord Gregory is ready to leave. He asked me to find you," replied Vijay.

The happy couple joined Vijay, and they were soon inside a horse-drawn closed carriage with Lord Gregory waiting inside. The carriage was followed by Lord Gregory's armored guards, mounted upon horses. The excited couple announced their good news to Lord Gregory.

Lord Gregory commented, "The two of you—Hughie and Andalusia, you make a lovely couple. And do look after young Vijay and ensure he loves cricket and gets an education and becomes a shining example in life. He may well play a critical role in making India—who knows?—the global cricket powerhouse and supervisor in two hundred years' time, perhaps?"

The convoy passed along Museum Road, at a site of construction of a Jesuit educational institution called St. Joseph's Boys European High School. They passed along Brigade Road and, by the next hour, were on the deserted tracks to the outskirts of Bangalore City, on their way to Lord Gregory's mansion. The sound of horses' hooves, nighttime insects, and the carriage wheels were the only accompaniment to the conversations the four had on their way home.

Lord Gregory said, "The Enchanted Willow saved the day today. I heard that Lord Clarkson lost a fortune to the match fixers."

"Would there be any chance of retribution?" asked Andalusia.

"Perhaps," replied Lord Gregory. "But I should think that the name of our game and its honor count most. In any case, that is a matter between the match fixers and the culprits, who don't deserve to be called cricketers." It was nightfall now, and they had passed a village along the dusty tracks, surrounded by farmland. The carriage began its slow circular ascent along the winding path carved off Nandi Hills, on top of which was located Lord Gregory's family estate and tea plantations.

"Where's that magical bat now?" asked Vijay.

"I prefer to address it as the Enchanted Willow," said Lord Clarkson. "It's already in the possession of Errol, who collected the bat from me after the match. You see, cricket was essentially a game invented by shepherds in England as they hit a rounded object with their sticks. It later evolved into a cricket bat and ball and is today a well-recognized sport in His Majesty's empire. The Shepherds are still the informal founders and guardians and custodians of cricket, and we are very pleased to see the growth of this game from its humble beginnings of hitting a stone across the moors with our canes to what it is now. We are very proud that cricket is now officially governed by the Marylebone Cricket Club in London. We are even more proud that it has spread to the Indian subcontinent, the Caribbean, and Australia, thus far."

"Where do you see the sport reaching in, say, two hundred years' time from now?" asked Hugh.

Lord Gregory glanced across to Vijay and answered, "I see the day when your country, Vijay, can be the center of cricket in the world, when the game spreads to far and across the globe—to the Far East, to South America. I do believe that we may have a shortened version of the game, played over one day, instead of its present format of over four to five days. I see it having a lot of financial future. But for now, if I can rid the game of match fixers, I would be so much happier.

"The Shepherd's Triad will live on for hundreds of years, and I would like to see our descendants looking after our noble game in centuries to come and—hopefully, like today, when the honor of our noble game gets threatened—to use the Enchanted Willow for such special purposes."

The carriage had by now reached the middle portion of its ascent up the winding roads of the hills. Andalusia heard the horses neigh, and the whole carriage rocked and came to an abrupt halt. "What's going on?" asked Lord Gregory.

One of the guards rode forward and then returned, with a steely look in his eyes. "We're under attack, my lord. Looks like bandits. Only—they are English."

"What?" uttered Lord Gregory. "I must see this to believe it." He hastily jumped out of his carriage and stared in the direction forward. The cliff road formed a precipice and was a few thousand feet above ground level.

He saw over two dozen men, with their faces in masks and carrying torches. They had Enfield rifles with bayonets and swords.

"Who are you? What's this little joke about? Explain yourselves!" shouted Lord Gregory.

"This isn't a joke, Lord Gregory, your worship," answered a voice from what appeared to be the leader of the group. "This is for real. You are under attack for stealing my money with your blooming magic bat."

"Who are you, you coward? Uncover your face, so we can see who you are. I haven't stolen anyone's money. I am willing to defend my honor, if need be, with a swordfight. A duel to the death."

"I know that voice," said Hugh. "It sounds like Lord Clarkson."

"'Tis right, laddie," replied the leader, as he slipped open his mask to reveal that it was indeed Lord Clarkson. "We fight till the death until I get my money back. The bookies have taken it all away. You are responsible for this. There will be blood."

Lord Gregory gave signals to prepare his guards for battle. "Action stations, take your positions."

"Wait," said a voice from behind. It was Andalusia. "Can we resolve this peacefully, without bloodshed?"

"No," said Clarkson. "You cost me so much money. I am a humiliation in my team's dressing room. This news has yet to reach England. I am now permanently disgraced. I cannot leave India now. I'm trapped here."

Another one of the attackers removed his mask—it was Harold Wellington. "We have that so-called Enchanted Willow in our possession. We found this Shepherd colleague of yours. He was quite stupid, really."

Two of the masked men produced a corpse wrapped in a white cloth. They threw it across the ground in front of them. The cloth opened, and the lifeless body of a man rolled onto the ground. Lord Gregory recognized the body as the second member of the Shepherd's Triad.

"We asked him to politely give us the bat. He was expecting us to spare his life. I'm afraid we are not so merciful tonight. Not after what that bat did to us," said Lord Clarkson.

Wellington brandished the magic cricket bat. He placed it on the ground. He took a large woodcutter's axe and chopped off the bottom third and threw it across to Lord Gregory. "Is this what it is—some bloody piece of wood that ended our reputations? There will be bloodshed. You'll pay dearly for this."

They charged forward with bayonets pointed to attack the convoy. It was about a dozen masked men against an even number of Lord Gregory's forces. It was nightfall, and the clash between the swords of men, only illuminated by the light of surrounding torches, was all too frightening for Andalusia. She was asked by Hugh to hide behind the carriage, but she sneaked across, beside the rocks across the battle scene. She found the partly chopped Enchanted Willow on the ground and picked up the larger piece.

She grabbed it and then felt a strong grip across her arm. It was Brian Cashman. "You whore. You dare think you can get away with what your fiancé did this afternoon?"

Andalusia screamed; this was heard by Lord Gregory and Hughie, who were both engrossed in close-combat bayonet fighting. Hugh dropped his bayonet and ran toward Andalusia.

He saw Andalusia holding the larger piece of the Enchanted Willow, but in the whole-arm grip of Brian Cashman standing behind her and with a knife across her throat.

"If you take one foot forward, I'll slit your little poppet's throat," growled Cashman.

"Let her go, Brian. You can have me instead," reasoned Hughie.

The close-combat bayonet battle now came to a freeze in response to this new development. Lord Gregory intervened, "Mr. Cashman, I shall offer you enough money if you let go of the lady safely and leave us to go home. The bat had nothing to do with it. It was the brilliant ability of Hugh Dawson that won us the game."

"Don't you sweet-talk me, pockmark," said Cashman. "I know what did it. Consider the second life lost, you stuttering Shepherd."

"I will always love you, Hughie," said a terrified Andalusia.

Cashman pressed the blade of the large knife closer to Andalusia's throat. Suddenly, a gunshot was heard from the distance, coming from above the hills. It was Lord Gregory's reinforcements—his house servants, worried at the delayed return of their master, had organized help.

"Let her go, and scatter, you lot!" bellowed Gregory. "You have nowhere to escape. We are still allowing you to go unharmed."

"You'll let the Crown's authority know of this, no doubt," replied a defiant Lord Clarkson. "Not so easy, we fight to death."

"It's your entire fault, Cashman!" screamed Wellington. "This is strictly between us and Gregory. I was an honest man. Now I have blood on my hands. I should never have mixed in your company. Look what it has landed me in now." He aimed his rifle at Cashman and shot him straight in the forehead— Cashman, still gripping Andalusia and the Enchanted Willow, took a step backward and fell into the ravine several hundred feet below, taking Andalusia with him.

The bloodcurdling scream of Andalusia cut through the thick night.

"No!" screamed Hugh as they ran forward, only to see the lifeless body of the love of his life, Andalusia, at the bottom and the Enchanted Willow a fair distance away from her. The confusion made the attackers flee, and Lord Gregory and Dawson made the painful descent, in darkness, to retrieve Andalusia's body.

The next day, a British state funeral was held for Andalusia, who was to later gain the posthumous title of Dame Andalusia.

Wellington, Clarkson, and the rest of the attackers, were arrested by the Crown's police force and sentenced appropriately. Hugh Dawson, though, was inconsolable. He was to later return to England.

Chapter 3

Lord's Cricket Ground, London, June 2010

The home of cricket was bathed in glorious summer-solstice sunshine. It was eight p.m., the sun still shining brightly. Lord's had a full house today. The first of the best-of-three matches between the Amateurs XI and the Professionals XI was coming to a close.

This was a Twenty20-format cricket tournament developed by the billionaire Dawson Brothers Company. It was essentially an exercise to challenge the notion of whether amateurs were better or worse than professionals in Twenty20 cricket. It was a well-known fact that one-day cricket, which consisted of one hundred overs bowled and played across seven hours in a day, and Test cricket, played across six hours and ninety overs bowled for each of five days, could only be played by skillful professionals. Professional cricketers who had to first prove themselves at lower grades of cricket, such as club cricket and first-class cricket, before they caught the eye of the national selectors to warrant selection to play for their country. But this tournament was to explore the possibility of amateur Twenty20 cricketers, who did not necessarily have as much professional cricket experience, needing to be as skilled as their professional counterparts when it came to the shortest format of the game, namely, 20/20 cricket.

Twenty20 cricket, also called T20 or simply 20/20, is played over barely three to four hours, with a total of forty overs bowled in the full match, shared equally by the two competing teams. Fast scoring and big hitting of the ball are encouraged. It has taken the world by storm in this decade and had contributed to the rise and fall of at least two of its entrepreneurs so far—one in the USA in 2009 (Texas billionaire Sir Allen Stanford) and the other in India in 2010 (Lalit Modi, who watched Major League Baseball in the USA in the 1980s and imported that model into India and used it on 20/20 cricket).

International Test Cricket has been in existence since 1879 and one-day cricket since 1970, while 20/20 cricket, the latest and shortest format, since 2005. Twenty20 cricket is sometimes looked down upon by connoisseurs of the game, who believe that Test Cricket, the five-day version of the sport and its purest original version, is its only true form. But the busy twenty-first-century lifestyles of the paying public meant that 20/20 cricket gets preferred over Test cricket, as a full match could get completed in only three to four hours. It catered to a younger audience, making it globally easy to advertize as a form of cricket to be adopted by non-cricket-playing countries.

It also seems to be the cause of the likely demise of the one-day game as well. And the vast numbers of annual global 20/20 tournaments worldwide means that the days of one-day cricket, and perhaps also of five-day Test-match cricket, may well be numbered.

Then there was the shift in global financial control of the sport.

The Imperial Cricket Council, with its headquarters at the Lord's stadium in London, was the previous governing body for cricket. This British-colonial-era name, since 1909, was subsequently changed to the International Cricket Council in 1965. It presently has ten main member countries as full members—England, Australia, India, Sri Lanka, the West Indies, South Africa, Zimbabwe, New Zealand, Pakistan, and Bangladesh. It helps govern cricket worldwide and organizes cricket matches globally. It helps the remaining new countries to cricket—105 of them, known as the affiliates, as varied as the United States of America to Afghanistan—to develop into competitive cricket nations. But things are not as rosy as they sound.

The Board of Control of Cricket in India, the BCCI, currently has the highest income of any national cricket board. Its income has increased manifold in 2007 and 2008 and crossed 217 million US dollars, as compared to 141 million US dollars in 2006-07, leading to a surplus of 65 million US dollars. The global media rights for international cricket to be held in India between March 2010 and March 2014 were awarded to Nimbus for US$612 million. Official kit sponsorship rights for five years from 2010 to 2013 inclusive were awarded to Nike for US$43 million. Air Sahara became the official sponsor for the Indian team, for a period of four years, at a cost of US$70 million. That's not counting another US$450 million from the sale of other rights, including hotel, travel, and ground sponsorship.

As India is by far the biggest market in terms of cricket's international revenue, the BCCI's opinions tend to gain a large weighting within the ICC's decision-making process, with other cricketing nations unwilling to oppose due to the potential loss of financial benefits associated with Indian cricket. The ICC changed location too—from the traditional headquarters of cricket at Lord's in London to Dubai in the Middle East in 2005.

All this was unknown to the gorgeous Amelia Kanowski, the last-minute replacement for the regular cricket reporter of the newspaper and website, *Evening Chronicles*. Essentially a fashion journalist, she was wearing a lavender three-quarter-sleeved jersey top, with elasticized gathers at the bust and cuffs and matching jeans to go with her high-heeled shoes.

She was six feet tall, intelligent, had blue eyes, brown hair up to her neck, an athletic figure, tanned skin with a light brownish hue, long manicured nails, and well-shaped teeth behind a luscious pair of lips. Free spirited, with a positive attitude to life, she was enjoying the tunes of Lady Gaga's hit song "Telephone" playing back to her through her iPhone. She heard her iPhone ringtone interrupt the Lady Gaga melody and hastily gathered it from her handbag as the London Underground Tube train neared St. John's Wood Station. She disembarked, amidst the hurried Londoners, to the sounds of the public announcement announcing characteristically, "Mind the gap," and could hear the voice of her boss, Graham, on the other end.

"Are you there yet? The match is nearing completion and has gone against all expectations. We were expecting the world's finest Professional Cricketers XI to easily beat the inexperienced Amateurs XI, but it has turned out exactly the opposite—the amateurs are about to claim a huge victory over the professionals."

The background noise of the Tube Station was too loud for Amelia to be able to hear her boss. She replied, "I'm walking into the media box," and hung up. She walked across the road to enter the stadium and used her journalist's pass to enter the Lord's media box. The Lord's media center was the first aluminum, semimonocoque building in the world. Built in 1999, it can house close to two hundred journalists and commentators for watching and reporting cricket.

Amelia, of Prussian descent, did not really understand the game of cricket. Raised in soccer-crazy Europe and primarily a fashion journalist, she was the last-minute replacement for the regular sports journalist of her newspaper. The match was so one-sided and the result so opposite in its expected outcome that all the reporters in the media box were furiously typing away the results on their laptops. They all seemed too busy to notice Amelia.

She saw the giant electronic scoreboard. It read, "Professionals XI 181/9 in 20 overs, Amateurs XI 175/3 in 18.2 overs," and she did not understand what that meant. How could her heartless boss send her to report a game, at last-minute notice, in this manner?

She saw the players on the field. It had a young Indian batsman at the crease, whom the whole stadium was cheering for, and an Australian cricketer at the other end.

She worked out their names from the scoreboard as Amay Indulkar and Dean Delaney. She saw one of the opposition players bowl at Amay and Amay turn the ball around his hips and score a run and the stadium erupt in a standing ovation and cheer and the batsman wave his bat to the crowd in acknowledgment of their cheering. She saw his individual score change on the scoreboard from 99 to 100 runs. The next ball was bowled to the Australian batsman, Dean Delaney. She saw him come down the wicket and smash the ball over midwicket and the ball flying into the spectators. She saw his individual score touch 50 runs, the whole stadium standing up and clapping for the victorious Amateurs XI and the men at the press box clapping their hands in appreciation of this improbable, yet real, result.

The two batsmen shook hands with the opposition players and ran back to the dressing room pavilion, with stumps as souvenirs in their hands. She saw them take off their helmets and gloves. The shorter Indian batsman was barely five feet and six inches tall, in her estimation, and the taller Australian player was six feet tall. The whole stadium gave a standing ovation and cheers to all the players and clapped their hands as the sun set on this great cricket ground on a long London summer evening. Amelia needed her report. Her boss wouldn't forgive her if she did not produce one by this evening. She switched on her iPhone and noted several Wi-Fi connections to choose from. She clicked a few more buttons, paid the necessary fee, and was soon able to use the local area network. She had an application program called Spear—a viral software application designed to read other reporters' articles across the LAN and with intelligent-enough software to borrow the relevant lines of each reporter's articles and subsequently synthesize a report on its own. Spear was her secret weapon to use whenever her boss sent her to cover events that she was not primarily trained in. She downloaded a couple of articles written by other reporters, and Spear did the rest, synthesizing a match report of two hundred words in barely three minutes. She quickly switched off her iPhone and decided to leave.

She just remembered—she needed a photo of the match too! She took out her digital camera and wandered down toward the presentation area. One last photograph and then cricket would be out of her life forever.

She stood by the other reporters and journalists at the presentation area. Former West Indian great fast bowler Michael Holding, master of ceremonies, dressed in a smart suit and shades, appeared at the Lord's balcony presentation area.

He spoke in his characteristic voice, well-known the world over to women watching cricket in their living rooms and making them all drool in appreciation of it. "Ladies and gentlemen, we have witnessed an amazing new experiment on cricket. It has been debated all decade, ever since the start of the shortest version of the game, namely, 20/20 cricket, whether the amateurs would be able to match international professionals. We have the chance to find out in these best-of-three matches. It appears, so far, that the amateurs can play just as well as the professionals. This is a big victory for the game and a significant step forward in marketing our sport to all the corners of the world. Three cheers for cricket."

The crowd gave three huge cheers to this announcement.

"But, ladies and gentlemen, we have to announce the winners of this contest today, where the amateurs won an easy victory over the professionals. We can't wait for the remaining two matches to see who wins this series."

She saw the Amateur XI's captain, Chris Dawson, come to the podium, get briefly interviewed by Michael Holding, and accept his winning check from the sponsors. He then called the losing captain of the Professionals XI and then, after he had received his check, watched the man of the match, Amay Indulkar, appear and accept his check. Amelia clicked a few photographs on her digital camera.

She walked into the maze of corridors through the Lord's stadium, looking for a way out. She had her report; she had a few photographs. It was time to leave.

She saw the corridors adorned with paintings over three hundred years old of several cricketers from the past. This ground was steeped in history. She saw names and portraits of Jack Hobbs, Dr. W. G. Grace, C. B. Fry, Leonard Hutton, and Sir Donald Bradman—all of which did not seem to make any sense to her. She was on her way out—but could not find an exit.

Out of the corner of her eye, she caught the figure of a young Indian lady, dressed in a blue *salwar kameez*, who was followed by two burly six-foot Indian men in suits and sunglasses, whom she presumed were her bodyguards. Amelia could hear a tearful sob from this exotically gorgeous Indian lady. She seemed to be crying; Amelia noticed a tear running down her cheek and a partially wet tissue paper in her hand. Her facial expression and body language spoke of a broken heart.

She then saw a man appear from the door from which the lady and her bodyguards had emerged. It was the same Indian man who had scored those hundred runs earlier and had won the man-of-the-match award. He was clean shaven, with black eyes and black hair, and stood, heartbroken and motionless, watching the Indian beauty walk away from him. There appeared to be another man, with dark glasses, a French beard, and a suit, standing behind Amay Indulkar, waiting to talk to him.

She decided to click one last close-up photograph. After all, this man was the star of the show today. She clicked a quick photo, which also captured other people in the room.

One of the Lord's Cricket Ground stewards approached Amelia and asked, "Excuse me, madam, can I see your permit and identification please?" Amelia took out her journalist's permit. The steward studied the permit superciliously. "We only allow journalists into the media box with that pass—not into the Long Room. This is the Long Room area, reserved for honorary members of the Marylebone Cricket Club and players. I'm afraid I have to ask you to please leave the premises from that exit. I'm sorry," said the steward courteously.

Amelia was shown the exit, and she thanked the steward and left the ground. She was only too keen to leave. She walked toward the Tube Station. She had her report and pictures for her boss. She was off to Paris the following day to cover the Victoria's Secret lingerie fashion show. At least this was her real area of expertise in journalism and fashion photography. She couldn't wait for the start of the show in Paris to see the latest fashion giants clothe beauties in the laciest of bikinis and coat them in angelic feathers, with music, wine, and celebrity glitterati. Cricket was clearly not her cup of tea—her stand-in job for the cricket reporter was just over, anyway. She walked down to the St. John's Wood Tube Station and took the first train home.

Chapter 4

The New Scottand Gard

The next day, Amelia, fully packed for her flight to Paris, waltzed into her office in red high-heeled shoes and a red cutout sleeveless dress with a square neckline and a fitted bodice, up to midthigh length, that revealed her trim and tall figure to the outside world. Her high-heeled shoes clicked at each step as she entered her boss's office and handed him a USB drive that contained last evening's cricket report. She had edited the other reporters' report of the match into her own, with subtle alterations, not large enough to be picked up by the public if they were to read her report and another reporter's. Spear was her own little secret weapon.

Amelia declared to Graham, "I have come to pick up my tickets. I'm sure you have received an e-mailed report and pictures of the match last evening. I'm all set for a very fashionable weekend in Paris."

Graham replied, "Amelia, we need to have an important talk, may I see you in private? I think you might have missed the other big news."

Amelia froze. She only hoped that this would not interrupt her keenly anticipated trip to Paris. Nobody at the office knew about Spear. The present global financial crisis could not possibly have caused her boss to lay her off work.

Graham, in a somber tone, remarked, "It has been reported overnight that the coach of that Amateurs XI winning team appears to have been . . . murdered at his hotel room last night."

"Really? By whom? Do you know?" She was shocked to have come so close to a crime, yet it looked all so innocent yesterday.

"The police are investigating this. After all that's happened in cricket lately, the authorities believe that this may be the work of match fixers," replied Graham.

"Match fixers?" asked Amelia. "But the game looked so clean."

"The police have been phoning every newspaper and Internet news office that covered the match yesterday. This is to gather as much evidence as they can. Every person at the ground, every piece of the match footage and, regrettably, every photograph taken may have to be analyzed by them. This is where you come in. It is to help them spot clues as to any match fixers on the ground that day, whose picture may have been captured by chance, which may help bring the perpetrators to justice," replied Graham.

"On a good note, I have to say that this won't interrupt your trip to Paris. I'll be handing over your USB drive to the police this morning, and they may contact you later, if need be. It seems, though, very unlikely that they will contact you, but I just thought I'd let you know about all of this, as your employer," concluded Graham.

Amelia was a touch flustered at all the fuss. She was really sorry to hear the news about the coach's death. But the thought of her photos being analyzed by the police made her departure to Paris a bittersweet experience.

The New Scotland Yard's toxicology crime branch head, Professor and Chief Inspector Sir Nigel Harrison, was at his desk, glancing over the scores of e-mails sent from all the newspapers and journalists of all the pictures they had taken. He was barely into the twelfth e-mail in his inbox and still had nearly two hundred more to go through. But it was already midday, and he was seriously behind target.

He picked up his phone and spoke to his secretary, "Hey, Julie, I'm behind the eight ball in this Dawson case. Be a dear and get me a cup of tea with sugar and milk, if you would please."

Five minutes later, he heard a knock on his door. He was expecting Julie to enter with a soothing hot cup of tea. Instead, it was an unexpected and rather unwanted visitor. He recognized the man in the suit instantly. He was expecting a phone call or an e-mail from this person to schedule a meeting—but not in person and so unannounced.

Julie looked at him with a helpless look on her face. "Believe me, sir, I have tried, but—"

"Never mind, Julie," said Inspector Harrison as the imposing visitor entered the room.

He was six-and-a-half feet tall and had a large oval face. He was bald, with gray hair on the sides, with thick glasses, and a steely look in his eyes. He was the richest billionaire in the UK at the time. He was followed in by his life-size robot, his mobile humanized android secretary, Skittle. Skittle was a robot manufactured in Japan using artificial intelligence technology. It had a female form and could walk as fast as a normal human being. It had black eyes and carried a computer console in its hands and had a computer screen instead of a bust. It was able to talk and understand commands. It could take e-mails, listening to spoken voice, and could print, copy, and fax papers. A versatile walking computer of a robot working as a secretary.

The man, though, was Hedwig Dawson. He was the most powerful and feared businessman in all the UK. A veritable human shark, he could make or break companies—and with it, thousands of jobs and livelihoods—with one swift decision. He was intimidating, fast moving, highly intelligent, innovating— in one phrase, not someone to cross. Aged fifty-eight years of age and dressed in a double-breasted black suit, he appeared rushed and impatient, which was well-known to the world to be his usual self.

The Dawson Brothers Company, who organized this three-match 20/20 cricket series, consisted of Hedwig Dawson, the oldest brother; Orson Dawson, the middle brother, who was widely regarded as a middle-aged millionaire playboy; and the youngest brother, Graeme Dawson, who was the kindest and most virtuous of the three.

They were direct descendants of ancestor Hughie Dawson from his marriage to another woman after he had moved back to England from India in 1810. While Hedwig and Orson went into the business and corporate world, Graeme Dawson took up club and county cricket and, after retirement, turned into a cricket coach. Graeme used some of his inherited wealth to fund medical research. He also happened to be the coach of the Amateurs XI, and it was his murder case that the toxicology department was presently investigating.

Hedwig roared at Inspector Harrison, "Well, I have no time for handshakes or pleasantries! Have you caught the criminals who performed this dastardly act on my brother or not?"

His android secretary is a perfect foil to his cold demeanor, thought Harrison. The android, in full human form, with black artificial hair manufactured into the hairstyle of a page boy, white artificial skin, and brown eyes, still had a vacant look when staring at real human beings. If it wasn't for the prior knowledge that Skittle was an android, it could easily be mistaken for a live human being if you passed it in the street.

"We're working on it," said Harrison. "We have one suspect, and we are tracing the lead as to where the suspect may have come from. One of the cricketers of the Amateurs XI was approached by a bookmaker after the match. So overall, we may be able to find out fairly soon and get to the bottom of this regrettable incident."

"Enough of your extravagant words, you could have just said no!" screamed back Dawson. "I'll get my solicitors to call you within the next hour and arrange cooperation with my own special security forces and private detectives. They will solve the crime faster than you lot. For all you know, the perpetrators may already have left the country and may be far away, laughing at us, on another continent."

With those words, he left in a huff, accompanied by his android mobile secretary. Julie Hamlet entered the room and asked Inspector Harrison, "Are you all right, sir?"

"Yes, thanks," said a visibly shaken Inspector Harrison. "That's just his personality. Just get me my former colleague at the Greater Manchester toxicology unit, Inspector Bob Davidson, urgently on the phone please."

Chapter 5

Bob Davidson

That same evening, the red-colored Virgin Voyager train pulled into London Euston station. In it was Inspector Bob Davidson, responding to the distress call from his colleague, Inspector Harrison.

Davidson was aged fifty with brown hair interspersed with gray hair and a lock of it on the left side, had brown eyes, was six feet tall, and had a slightly overweight build.

He took the Tube from Euston to Enfield and read the *Evening Standard* papers about the abrupt end of the life of an innocent man, a well-loved cricket coach, and the match-fixing conspiracy theories. He had read the official e-mails sent to him from Inspector Harrison earlier. He knew that this was going to be the biggest case of his career.

By six p.m., he was in the headquarters of the London Toxicology Department. He was met by an eager Inspector Harrison.

"Bob, how are you? Am I glad to see you, my dear fellow! I have a real situation on my hands. I am simply unable to solve it. I have the Department of Crime Prevention breathing down my throat to come up with a solution to this high-profile crime. I barely slept for an hour last night, after this murder took place. I have obtained permission from Her Majesty's government to allow you to work on this case with me."

"Nigel, won't you take some rest? It's all right. I'll take things from here. We can meet tomorrow, dear friend," said Davidson, upon seeing the fatigued eyes of his peer.

"There are few things I need to tell you first, Bob. It won't take a few moments. I badly need a drink—let's quickly debrief, then . . . I'll leave."

They walked into Harrison's office. They both shared a glass of cognac.

"How much do you know of what's going on, Bob? Or at least how much are true, what are the fibs, and who are the protagonists?"

"Only so much. That the good Coach Graeme Dawson was murdered in cold blood, but not much else, really. That his big brother, the ruthless billionaire, extremely politically connected, has got his private detectives onto the case. That the unknown murderers are still at large. There are huge sums of money involved. And there are match fixers probably involved as well."

"It's a bit of a sudoku puzzle, Bob," said a tired Harrison, with worry lines etched across his brow. "Let's start from the beginning."

Sir Nigel began to explain, "Ever since 2004, when international and domestic premier-league Twenty20 cricket first began, it caused a lot of financial success across India, the Caribbean, England, Australia, and South Africa, worth billions of dollars. For instance, the first Indian Premier

League that was staged in India in 2008 changed the face of the game. The league involved over hundreds of players contracted and over billion dollars investment.

"Two people in the past who earned fame have also had their reputations spoiled in this game. It seems to have the nasty habit of putting down those who make money out of it. 20/20 is such a huge money-spinner—and money is the root of all evil.

"Now, the Dawson Brothers Company is the chief sponsor and organizer of this event. They have long been patrons towards cricket and have dedicated huge sums of money over their two-hundred-year history towards development of the game around the world.

"So they organized this 20/20 best-of-three match tournament to showcase an internationally mixed Amateurs XI—people who have never played professionally before, as they have other interests and other jobs. They decided to match this team with professional cricketers, again, chosen internationally. The professionals play all three formats of the game—the longest version, namely, Test cricket; the middle version, namely, one-day cricket; and the shortest version, namely, 20/20 cricket.

"So far so good, but when 350 billion pounds in revenues and sponsor fees can be potentially lost on account of disbanding this tournament, it can be very worrisome for the chief organizers—the Dawson brothers. Not to mention an international incident of multinational proportions, because each member of each of the two teams has been chosen from each of the ten Test cricket—playing nations.

"Two significant events have occurred after the conclusion of the first match at Lord's. One was the declaration by the star batsman and man of the match, Amay Indulkar, that he had been approached by a bookmaker to fix his score and throw his wicket away for a cheap score of runs for the next two games or risk losing his and his family's lives. The second was the murder of the coach. It seems like the two are connected and that the match fixers *may* have killed the coach, but we can't be too sure as we have no evidence.

"The good news is, Coach Graeme Dawson is *not* actually dead. He is alive—in suspended animation."

Davidson listened to all the evidence narrated by Inspector Harrison attentively. Suspended animation is the slowing of life processes by external means without termination. Breathing, heartbeat, and other involuntary functions may still occur, but they can only be detected by artificial means.

"This is how we, at toxicology, got involved. The media was told that he'd died in order to make the real culprits think that they had succeeded.

"Our job is to find out how he ended up in suspended animation. We know that Graeme worked with suspended animation technology in his research labs—but why do it on himself, if he indeed did do it to himself, and why on that night? The detectives at the scene have failed to find any pertinent clues towards the culprits. I'll make sure you get a chance to analyze the hotel tapes and the evidence.

"The Amateurs XI have, expectedly, disbanded. They fear more bookmakers will approach them with similar death threats. They are actually expatriates living in all corners of the British Isles, in full-time employment in other jobs. The trouble is, the coincidence of this probable attempted murder and the death threats to the star player have made others think twice about playing for the Amateurs XI. It takes a lot of weeks, to months, of preparation and organization for such a tournament. The professionals have to, rightfully, return back to their own countries and play the game professionally for their countries and cannot spend any more time beyond the thirtieth of June for the conclusion of this tournament. The loss of television rights and broadcast rights with the disbandment of the tournament will result in a cataclysmic loss of money for Hedwig Dawson.

"This is why he is super keen to solve the case as of yesterday. But we have pursued all leads without success. My secretary, Julie, shall show you the evidence collected," concluded Inspector Harrison.

"You know, Nigel, one last thing. You know who would really be useful in a situation like this?" asked Inspector Davidson.

"I don't know, Bob, who?"

"Landon," replied Inspector Davidson.

"You mean Landon Beau?" asked Harrison. "He abandoned the force ages ago. I know it was a personal tragedy that befell him and my late daughter, but neither he nor we could have prevented what had happened."

"Nevertheless, I was thinking of him on my train ride down here. He seems to have the perfect skills for this kind of job. He should be about twenty-eight years old by now. He was one of our best undercover officers. He was trustworthy and loyal to the force. And above all, he was a former English club cricketer," replied Davidson.

"I hear what you are saying, but won't there be problems getting Landon to work with us again? I know him personally as well," said Harrison.

"I'm aware of that, Nigel. I'll work on that. For now, you go and get some rest, old fellow. I'll take the case from here."

Later that night, Julie approached Bob Davidson. "Mr. Davidson, I have located him. He's in Greater Manchester, of all places, believe it or not! Lives in Wigan, in the suburb of Hindley Green, post code WN2 4SZ, and drives a pacific-blue-colored Volvo S40 car, with registration plates T-325-JKU. He's working in a security firm called Spyware, and I've got his direct mobile phone number—it's 079-3246-1638. Would there be anything else you would need, Mr. Davidson?"

"Good work, Julie, and thanks for everything. I'll get onto the first train tomorrow for Wigan to meet our man."

Chapter 6

Landon Beau

The next day, on an overcast Lancashire day, Inspector Davidson disembarked the train off Wigan North Western Station and hailed a taxi to the peaceful suburb of Hindley Green. He arrived there by 9:00 a.m. into Spyware Stores, right on time, as the front door opened for the day's business. He couldn't help thinking of all the great times he had when working with Landon Beau over ten years ago. Back in 2000, when Landon was eighteen, he was considered the best junior detective in the force, cracking cases involving small-time drug dealers and burglars with ease.

His life looked set for greatness when he met his partner, Sabrina. Sabrina was pregnant at the time of Landon's last mission—to locate a match fixer in the Leeds area for the then—Hansie Cronje match-fixing scandal. Landon located his target, caught up with him, and arrested him. But he was threatened with dire consequences by the bookmaker, who openly declared this en route to jail.

Sabrina and her unborn child passed away the same evening that he had caught the match fixer. The tragic occurrence after that mission made Landon retire from the police force and choose selling security gadgets for homes as his primary occupation. Landon was particularly critical of the work schedules of the force and did not intend any further contact with the police force after that incident.

Davidson entered the store. It had a young female employee, who told Davidson that Landon was at home for most of the day.

He felt a bit nervous phoning the former rising star of the police force. What if Landon slammed the phone down on him, especially after the tragic events of 2000? Had Landon forgotten and forgiven?

He dialed the number provided to him by Julie. No reply. But it reached Landon's answering machine; the voice was definitely Landon's. Davidson did not leave a message. Davidson had Landon's home address and set across the town center toward Leigh Road.

Davidson knocked on the door of 29 Leigh Road. He heard the footsteps of the occupant walking downstairs. The door opened. Davidson was delighted to see his former colleague again. He had his casual navy blue long-sleeved sweater on, formal white shirt, with collar out of the neckline, a short haircut, blue eyes, clean shave, and dark-brown trousers, with formal black boots.

"Who is it, sir? Can I help you?" replied the young man, not recognizing his former colleague in the force.

"I'm Inspector Davidson from the police force. I am so pleased and honored to see you again, Landon, after all these years. I hope you are well."

"Oh, hello, Inspector Davidson! It has been a long time, indeed. Please do come in," answered the young man courteously. *He does not seem to harbor any anger from the past, from his initial demeanor*, thought Harrison.

Over a cup of tea, they caught up on old times. "We still remember how well you solved the Bolton and Bury drugs case in 1999. And the illegal immigrant racket in the Merseyside area—stuff of legend for an eighteen-year-old," recalled Inspector Davidson.

"I just did my job at the time," replied a humble Landon.

"Err, Landon, there was a little bit more than just reminiscing on old times that brought me here today."

"Was it to do with me joining that force again? Not happening, I'm afraid. Your department is detrimental towards my well-being," said Landon.

"Landon, what happened ten years ago was a long time ago. It happened and it was unfortunate and—"

Landon interrupted, "She died, Inspector, she died. My child died with her. End of story."

"Landon, it wasn't your fault. There was nothing you could have done to have prevented it," replied Davidson.

"Yes, it's called joining the police force and working like a naive lapdog. This meeting is over. Thank you for calling in, but if it's for another case, forget it," retorted Landon.

"Landon, I'll leave now. But remember, I do have something special to say. I know that you love cricket. Well, this time, the name of cricket is in jeopardy. A game you have a passion for—and a game that I know you can play well. If I know one law enforcement officer, past and present, who is most perfectly suited for this task at hand, it's you. I have only ever made such an appearance once in ten years thus far. It's that rare," said Davidson.

"The damage is already done. I lost my wife and unborn child. I won't be making the same mistake again," answered an irritated Landon.

"Landon, I cannot say any more, except that I wish you well. But what if I told you that you might find love again on this mission?" said Davidson in desperation.

Davidson hoped he was right. He did find that sometimes, whatever he spoke with true belief really did happen.

"I'm going to go now. I've got to chase a lot of leads in this mission. This is the reason I took up a desk job at the force now as I'm getting a bit too old for this running around and chasing leads. Remember that there's an old saying in our country. 'Everything happens for a reason.' You're rejoining the force for one mission that will involve you playing two 20/20 cricket games, one at the Oval and the other at Lord's, and possibly finding love again is well worth the effort," said Davidson as he bid Landon good-bye and left for London.

Amelia Kanowski was partying in Paris at the Victoria's Secret dance party that followed the fashion parade. She had a glass of champagne and was lost in the tunes of trance disco music, shaking her body alongside the Victoria's Secret models, compared to whom, she was as beautiful, if not more beautiful. She took several photographs that night and was only too keen to download them onto her laptop and, later on, e-mail them to her newspaper headquarters in London.

Amelia was unaware that she was being watched at the party. She had left her handbag on the marble chairs at the back end of the dance hall. The stranger detected her handbag and, wearing black gloves, opened it and found her digital camera within it. The stranger inserted a four-millimeter device into one of the charger ports. It shone in the darkness and blinked. It began downloading all her photographs into its small, four-millimeter frame. After three minutes, the download was complete. The stranger pulled out the device, placed Amelia's camera back into her handbag, and proceeded to covertly leave the club, leaving behind Amelia and the lingerie models on the dance floor, oblivious to what just took place.

Amelia reached her hotel room around three a.m. She was approached by several drunken male fashion designers for a one-night stand but rejected their amorous and lusty advances. She opened her handbag and checked her iPhone for messages. It was a text message from her boss, Graham, and several missed calls from her friends. The text message read, "Phone immediately—police believe you may have inadvertently captured vital evidence on camera—Graham." Amelia groaned at this message. Of all the photographs taken at the stadium, she had to be the one to capture evidence. Of all the nonsports journalists, she had to be asked to pick the short straw and cover that cricket game for the newspaper on that particular day. She cursed her luck.

She checked her e-mails over her Apple iPad. One of them was very well worded from an Inspector Davidson, asking her to call him as soon as she could for a friendly interrogation about where she got to take that photograph inside the stadium on the day of the match.

She decided to call the inspector the next day, after a proper bath and a good night's sleep.

She left her iPad on and went into the bathroom. She lit a few candles, closed the door behind her, and took her bathrobe off. The fragrance of the candles and glow of their pale light fell upon her body, highlighting her curves and femininity, her supple breasts, her long legs, and her wide hips. Amelia stepped into the bathtub filled with warm water and proceeded to cleanse herself.

An hour later, she emerged from the bath covered in a large towel. She put her nightwear on, dried her hair with a handheld dryer, took her mandatory daily oral contraceptive pill, and proceeded to catch up on some sleep.

Amelia did not sleep well that night. She felt a presence, like another person had intruded her privacy at some point in the recent past. She managed to convince herself that all was well and went back to sleep. She was soon in delta waves, dreaming of a handsome, dashing young detective, rescuing her from dangerous situations. Well, a girl could at least dream.

The next day, she awakened and, after freshening up, prepared to check out of the hotel. She checked out, choosing to skip breakfast, and was soon on a flight back home to London. She reached her home in London and decided to download all the images from her digital camera onto her iPad.

The phone rang at 29 Leigh Road. Landon, up to that point, was half undecided whether to pursue this mission. He did respect Davidson but harbored deep ill feelings for the police force from the incident of 2000. Landon Beau answered the phone. He heard another familiar voice from the past. It was his late fiancée's father. After a few minutes of conversation, he agreed to join Inspector Davidson on the mission to save cricket's name in its hour of need and to solve the case. He packed his bags and proceeded to catch the first train to London.

Chapter 7

Landon Beau in London

At their Enfield headquarters of the toxicology department, Julie Hamlet smiled and welcomed back Landon after ten long years. "So lovely to see you, Landon. I'm afraid there isn't enough time left. Inspectors Davidson and Harrison are with Hedwig Dawson in the round-table room."

They walked together to the meeting room. "Hedwig, as you know, needs no introduction. He has brought along his robotic secretary again. And we are expecting a visit from his executive secretary, the double-crossing Cindy Fartington. Inside the room are two of his private detectives as well to share in our case—Detectives Mork and Klumsy."

They opened the door, and Landon's eyes met with his former father-in-law, none other than Inspector Nigel Harrison, their first meeting in several years. It was of a father and a partner of a young lady common to them both, who had gone missing, so cruelly snatched from them both in the past.

Inspector Harrison introduced Landon to the room and said, "Landon, meet Lord Hedwig Dawson, the richest man in

Great Britain and foremost industrialist and chief executive director of this three-match cricket series. Meet his android secretary, Skittle, and his two private detectives who are also assigned to this case, Mork and Klumsy."

Landon recognized Mork and Klumsy. Both in their late forties, they were former antique hunters and policed the art world for fakes a decade ago. They were now in private detective work. They were known for their eccentricities. Mork was taller than Klumsy, and both wore identical spectacles and black suits. They were practically like brothers in arms.

Dawson roared, "This investigation of yours hasn't yielded a single clue. My private detectives are now legally obliged to gather information on this matter. I understand the only clue that you have so far is a photograph from a reporter on the ground and Mr. Indulkar's testimony about a match fixer. How pathetic. I'm sure my detectives will be able to solve the crime within the next three days."

Skittle projected a camera from the top of her head and took images of the meeting for filing.

"Did the search of the hotel room yield any clues at all?" bellowed Dawson.

Sir Nigel Harrison cautiously replied, "Yes, Mr. Dawson, we have a few clues of certain people who may have been with your brother Graeme before his unfortunate—"

Dawson interrupted, "The clues. I want to know the clues. What did you find?"

"I'm sorry, Mr. Dawson, but as I was about to get to the point, we have proof of the people in the tapes, entering his room, and are in the process of working out their identity."

The door opened. A bespectacled and slim middle-aged woman walked in, with gray and curly black hair up to her shoulders and early wrinkles on her face. She spoke in a Londoner's accent and introduced herself as Cindy Fartington. She sat next to Hedwig Dawson. "Cindy's my executive secretary, and I expect full cooperation with all that you find given to her."

The lights in the room dimmed, and the overhead projector's beam of the light, containing evidence of the case, flashed onto the whiteboard.

Sir Nigel Harrison formally began, "There are two separate people in the tapes. The first person is a humongous man, whose face is disguised in what looks like a balaclava and wearing gloves. He is seen on CCTV camera entering the room at 1917 hours. The coach must have been expecting him as he opens the door to the perpetrator's knock on the door, but the perpetrator, from his body language, does not bother introducing himself or shaking hands and seems to force his way in, rather than gently entering in the manner in which most guests do. He hurriedly leaves at 1949 hours. He takes an elevator, and it reaches the basement car park, from where he makes a getaway in a white minivan. This presumably was how he entered the hotel in the first place. We located the abandoned minivan far away from London, off the M62 highway bordering Yorkshire and Lancashire. It appears to have driven off the M62 into the Pennine Moors, where it was recovered by our team. The footsteps of the perpetrator were seen for ten yards on the ground before they disappear. Seemingly, he vanishes or, more plausibly, was picked up by an air vehicle, such as a helicopter."

Sir Nigel continued, "The second person is a known match fixer, accidentally captured in the photograph taken by a journalist at the Long Room at the stadium, following the conclusion of the first match. He was later seen on the hotel's CCTV images, entering the room, seemingly welcomed in, at 1925 hours, and leaving hastily at 1930 hours in a not-so-happy mood. In other words, he was present in the room soon after the coach was last known to be alive. Why he leaves within five minutes of entry is uncertain. We know who this second person is."

The images of a tall man in a balaclava and his entry into the room, along with the later arrival of the match fixer, were seen by the people in the room.

"And what else?" asked Dawson.

"And lastly and most bizarrely, inside the room, using our colorimetric techniques, as well as outside the minivan at the moors, we detected footprints of a size 20 shoe. It was a perfect match in terms of wear-and-tear pattern on both locations. It was likely to have been worn by the first perpetrator in a balaclava, given his tall body size.

"And perhaps what's most startling in this case is on Graeme himself. He's actually alive, in suspended animation, a sort of induced coma by means of hypothermia or an as-yet-unknown drug that we are trying to find."

"Satisfactory," muttered Dawson coldly. "I stand to lose over 350 million pounds in revenue if the perpetrators are not caught on time before the second match of the series, due in three days' time. Also, the team has largely disbanded. Cindy is in charge of the team's management as well, and my own son Chris is on the team as a bowling all-rounder. I have organized high-level security for the team. Remember, gentlemen, that I am very well connected in politics globally and in the UK. My pockets are so large that you can barely comprehend. I expect a full and swift resolution of this matter.

Cindy will provide you logistics on the type of players we will need as replacements and for security purposes."

Landon boldly spoke up at this point. "Mr. Dawson, if that's okay with you, could I be entrusted the responsibility of organizing the team to play the second match? You see, I was not such a bad batsman myself and . . ."

The cold silence engulfed the room. The seconds spent by Dawson as he contemplated this brave suggestion by Landon felt like hours. Harrison felt his head swelling and spinning around. How could Landon suggest anything to someone who just could not be negotiated with? Harrison felt that he should have warned Landon that the best attitude to dealing with Dawson is the salute-and-two-sacks-of-rice approach. Davidson felt his pulse rate rise, the visceral fear of the power of the rich and famous, and awaited the obvious outburst from Dawson.

To everyone's surprise, Dawson remained surprisingly open at the suggestion. He replied, "All right, you get only one match to pick and choose the team. They had better be of good, first-class-cricket quality. If they lose heavily, I will personally throw them all out. And consider that the end of your career."

Landon, always good at taking a mile when given an inch, went one step further. "I could open the batting with Indulkar. Inspector Davidson is not a bad bowler himself, and he could coach and play in the team as a player-coach. I know some friends of mine from university who are ex-club cricketers, who can play good cricket if asked to join. I'll leave for Manchester tomorrow and recruit them."

Fartington appeared concerned at these developments. "Hedwig, are you sure you know what you're doing? This young man's team is inexperienced and untested."

Dawson coldly replied, "Cindy, I listen to no one but myself. This young man has direction and purpose. I shall offer him one chance to put an Amateurs XI team in place, on the field, within the next three days. If that team fails to perform according to standards, I'll finish his career off as a law enforcement officer and cricketer."

He got up from the table, and his android secretary lowered the camera into its head, and the slits came back into place over its artificial hair. It then spoke, "Thank you for your time, ladies and gentlemen, but as you can see, Mr. Dawson is a very busy man, and his time is very precious." Her vacant stare and expression made the words all the more meaningless.

Dawson, Fartington, Mork, Klumsy, and the android, Skittle, left the room. Julie Hamlet entered to find the trio exhausted from the meeting. "How did it go?" she asked.

"We won!" exclaimed Harrison. "Young Landon here won us a big victory. Three cheers for felling Goliath!" And three throaty cheers were heard in the room toward Landon's bold suggestions to Dawson.

"Who is the lady—err—ladies?" asked Landon.

"Hedwig Dawson was courting women of the royal family and London's elite in the 1970s. He married the mother of his son, Chris Dawson, one of the cricketers of the Amateurs XI team. She mysteriously passed away in 2004. No cause of death was identified. She just sort of—wasted away," said Inspector Harrison.

"Cindy Fartington is actually his distant cousin and his executive secretary, very nasty lady, from my previous dealings with her. She is in charge of Dawson's metallic-ore mines in Eastern Europe—former countries of the USSR.

"As for Skittle—it's made in Japan. Hedwig's had it since his wife's death. He apparently purchased it in 2005. Hedwig is practically married to that thing twenty-four hours a day. I think I'll change the subject now because I know what you are all thinking when I said what I just said," said Harrison, with an impish smile on his face.

As they walked out in a jovial mood, Davidson asked Landon, "You made it in the nick of time. What made Inspector Harrison convince you to come over to London and join our case?"

Landon answered, "If there was one person in the world who knew Sabrina better than me, it was her own father, Inspector Nigel Harrison. He told me that her last few words to him before she passed away were that she wanted me to carry on with my life and not worry about hers and that it was not my fault that she was taken ill on that day that she died. He also wanted me to do it for him. So I was convinced."

Inspector Harrison's BlackBerry phone rang; the call was expected. It was Amelia, arranging for an urgent meeting the same day. They agreed to meet around seven p.m. that night.

Chapter 8

The Evidence

The present meeting between all the top law enforcement agencies in London was at the high-tech conference room at a converted underground leftover World War II air-raid bunker. It contained air-conditioned facilities, was extremely secret, and only accessible to the police. It contained a three-dimensional-image screen, conference tables, soundproof walls, and bright lighting.

There were forty people of Britain's top law enforcement officials in the room, including Landon Beau and Inspectors Davidson and Harrison. Inspector Sir Nigel Harrison stood at the main lectern and began to summarize the full case history to the audience. "The purpose of this meeting is to reiterate the evidence we have found pertaining to this case so far. We have the evidence divided into the following sections containing exhibits.

"The events of the night at the hotel. Graeme Dawson leaves the stadium and drives to his luxury five-star Bellingham Hotel room at Willesden Green by 1800 hours. I find it odd that such a dedicated coach would leave his team on the field during an actual match and go back to his hotel room. His team has been interviewed at length. Their verdict is that he had extensive faith in their abilities and that he told them that he was reportedly ill with a vomiting-like illness for weeks leading to this series. Concurrent reports from Mr. Hedwig Dawson also indicate that his youngest brother was recently not a very well man.

"The hotel front desk saw him entering around 1830 hours. He had his own swipe card, so he did not need to check in with them before entering.

"The hotel authorities confirm that, being such a busy hotel, they tend not to notice who enters the rooms sometimes. And the match fixer who entered at 1925 hours did not inform the front desk to contact the coach to open his door. That strikes me as being fishy from the start. The coach, or perhaps the tall perpetrator who entered earlier at 1917, actually allows the match fixer in after he knocks at the door. That seems to indicate to me that this meeting was prearranged. Further, this hotel does not have swipe cards that allow guests to access individual floors."

"Graeme Dawson was a man of enormous integrity. He was a former county cricketer and a well-respected coach in cricketing circles. Besides being a cricket coach, he was also a scientist working on discovering ways to preserve life by suspended animation. As far as his cricket was concerned, he would never fix a match for money. He played club cricket and county cricket for two decades and was actively involved in coaching cricketers from underprivileged countries. He was a real servant to the game and leaves behind a wife and two young daughters at university.

"The press have been told that he's dead. But actually, he's very much alive—in suspended animation. He may have well been poisoned by a substance that my toxicology department has yet to isolate, despite extensive tests.

"We believe that he was poisoned between 1917 to 1947 hours by the match fixer or tall balaclava-clad stranger or both that he had intentionally or unintentionally met with.

"So not only do we not have any motives as to why these people met with the Coach—one planned and one unplanned, as it appears—we also do not know what happened in the room. Was it an intended homicide, which went wrong or unfinished, resulting in suspended animation? We will never know.

"Another perplexing part of the full thing is the massive, size-twenty footprints we found in the room. The distance between each step indicates that we are dealing with a very, very tall person, around eight feet tall. This points to the balaclava-clad stranger

"Lastly, I haven't told Dawson or his private detectives about these two things. Firstly, it's an e-mail on Graeme's Sony VAIO laptop, which was found strewn across the room, along with other things around his body.

"It was found addressed to unknownx_27@hotmail. com. It looks as if he typed it just before he was attacked. We haven't yet contacted these people as we are awaiting further clues first as to who they are before we contact them. The recipient's Internet server has informed us that they have taken themselves off Hotmail, but their original details as to who it was registered with persist. It has been traced to a farmer in the Hampshire area called Jim Ayres. But no home address was found.

"Here's the e-mail in print:

> Dear Shepherd's triad,
>
> This is the hour of our greatest need.
> We are facing the gravest situation in
> the history of our noble game. I need
> this enchanted will—

"The e-mail abruptly stops there. The good thing was that he did not log off his e-mail account, so we have had access to all his previous e-mails, and our excellent cybercrime staffs have also obtained his passwords. We have searched through all of his e-mails and folders and junk mail and have not found a single e-mail addressed to these people previously. This raises the possibility as to whose 'will' was he after? Was he after some sort of inheritance from a dead relative?"

Landon was deep in thought. His mind was preoccupied by the thought of the word *enchanted will*. He was deep in thought, and five minutes later, it all clicked in. He excitedly screamed, "Eureka, I've got it!"

This abrupt outburst of an interruption to Inspector Harrison's lecture made all eyes in the whole room turn toward Landon. Landon made a statement. "Inspector Harrison, the e-mail appears to have been written incomplete. I have never heard of anything like an enchanted will. The word may have been incomplete. Could it simply be something else instead, such as the *Enchanted Willow*?"

He paused. He could feel everyone's eyes on him and their appreciation of his raw genius that made him such a promising intuitive young detective in the force several years earlier.

It was a paradigm shift—in the case, a quantum leap. Inspector Davidson was the first to burst out in congratulations. "Well done, Landon, you have just proven to yourself and to the rest that you are still an excellent police officer. Good form is temporary, but your class is permanent, as they say in cricket."

Inspector Harrison and the room were next to share their excitement. "Well done, Landon—you have just obtained a massive breakthrough that we needed in this case."

Julie Hamlet was unable to comprehend what was being discussed. "Nigel, what's this Enchanted Willow? What is it that you are all so excited about?"

Inspector Harrison explained, "The story of the Enchanted Willow and Mother Cricket are myths. They never really happened—no evidence—but we were taught not to cheat in the game as schoolkids by these myths. Let me explain. *Willow* is simply another name for a cricket bat. This myth about Mother Cricket and the Enchanted Willow in cricket goes around that there was once a great cricket match played a long time ago. It was plagued by cheaters—presumably match fixers. And then a magical object appeared that swung the match away from the match fixers."

"Mother Cricket?" asked Julie.

"Yes, it's a term used when cricketers start to bend the rules or cheat a little bit. That's when we warn that Mother Cricket is watching you. The main protagonist of that myth was a lady who died trying to defend cricket's honor. She died taking the Enchanted Willow with her to heaven, or at least most of it," said Harrison.

"Most of it. You mean, she left some behind on earth?" asked Julie.

"Yes," said Inspector Harrison. "The bottom third of this so-called magical cricket bat is presently in the museum of antiquities owned by Hedwig Dawson's younger brother Orson. The evil people who cheated on that day supposedly chopped the bottom third of this magical bat and preserved it on earth before it was taken to heaven. Or so the legend goes," replied Harrison.

"Orson Dawson, the infamous middle-aged millionaire playboy. How did he get it?" asked Julie

"They come from a cricketing family. Their forefathers played cricket in India and in England. It was obtained by someone along the line, we don't know who. And Landon has made a vital breakthrough in this case."

"How?" asked Julie.

"It appears that this Jim person might be a member of one of the most secret organizations in the world. It is believed that the Shepherd's Triad is a group of three shepherds who are the original custodians of cricket, responsible for looking after the game. Legend goes that there are three such people alive in the world at any given time—they always leave behind successors after their deaths. They keep in contact, and they save the game in its hour of need. They were believed, but without evidence, to have been involved in London and Australia in 1933, to outlaw bodyline fast bowling, and then again in 1979 to initiate the truce between Test cricket and World Series Cricket in Australia," said Harrison.

"Match fixing is like cricket's original sin, like a lusty, drunken nobleman after a maiden, always with defloration in mind. The Shepherd's Triad are like the knight in shining armor, always coming in to kill the drunken noblemen and save her honor. So the legend goes. I believe that we may have found credible evidence of the existence of the Shepherd's Triad in the twenty-first century. I was told this story as a child and did not believe that it could even exist—not until now. The evidence really looks like this legend is true after all and that we will be revealing it to the real world. How exciting! Like treasure hunting!" beamed an excited Harrison.

"It appears that the other piece of the Enchanted Willow or magic bat was what Graeme Dawson was after. He must have found the Shepherd's Triad and may have asked them for assistance in finding the magic bat," said Harrison.

"Jim might well be a modern version of this Shepherd's Triad. I don't know how Graeme came to know of him, but that's not important. The fact is that in all probability, from the evidence as it stands, Graeme sensed danger to his life or to the series before anyone else and tried to save it by getting in touch with the Shepherd's Triad. I know it's all a myth and legend and all that, but it appears that he has really got in touch with someone. This Jim person is a vital lead in the case," concluded Harrison.

Landon asked, "But, Inspector Harrison, hasn't any scientific tests been done on the piece of the Enchanted Willow so far, to demonstrate—err—magical properties?"

"Yes," he replied. "Scientists in several universities have studied Orson's bat. It's only a six-inch-by-three-inch-by-two-inch piece of wood and appears to have been chopped at an acute angle by some sort of sharp blade. It was studied by molecular specialists and quantum physicists and even subjected to the electron microscope and spectrometric studies. Nothing. Just an ordinary piece of wood. Cricketers have pieced it together to ordinary cricket bats and have not obtained any substantial results," replied Harrison.

"As for those footprints, do we have any leads?" asked Landon.

"Judging from the distance between the strides, they belong to someone who is eight feet tall. We have searched all our crime databases and haven't come up with anyone that tall. Except one consistent, probably unrelated, thing," said Harrison.

"Tell us, it may be important in unmasking the perpetrator," said Davidson.

"There was a series of unrelated mass strangling of sheep in New Zealand in 2002. The police there have on their records eyewitnesses' accounts of an eight-foot-tall humanoid, with massive hands and an electronic device that provided him an electronic voice. They traced the man a week later to a farm in Gore in the South Island. They have got his name in the system as Slocum," said Harrison.

"Slocum? Who's Slocum?" asked Landon Beau.

"Slocum is believed to be a former contract killer. He used to be linked to the Russian Mafia, who used him to strangulate the people who approached law enforcement officials. He was their chief assassin. His method of killing was strangulation using his bare hands. He could also break necks by his sheer muscle power. Apparently, this was a method of slaughtering sheep in the past, in the farm where he had been raised. He was never arrested, never photographed but believed to exist from testimonies from victims of the Russian-Chechnya war."

"So why did they abandon him?" asked Landon.

"That's for us to find out. He may well have been hired by someone else, for a higher price—who this someone is is yet undetermined," said Harrison.

Landon asked, "Inspector Harrison, what's the second thing you hid from Dawson but wished to tell us about the case?"

Harrison replied, "Just a small detail, probably not important. The smell of rotting eggs in the room. And the discovery of hydrogen sulfide capsules in the coach's pockets. Who manufactured them, we will never know. He appeared to have taken two of them—when, we can't confirm. Just adds to the mystery, really."

Harrison concluded, "May I just say one thing? This match is important. The honor of the game is at stake. The whole world knows that match fixers are at large to unsettle the Amateurs XI. We cannot let them win. We cannot afford to let negative thinking creep in.

"If there is nothing more to add, may I conclude this meeting and thank everyone for attending. Landon and Inspector Davidson, please come with me. We have to arrange a meeting with our star batsman, Amay Indulkar, in an hour's time."

"It's very timely," said Julie. "News from Taunton at a club cricket fixture—poor little Amay is out of form, dismissed for a first-ball duck. You have your task cut out in motivating him."

Chapter 9

Amay Indulkar — India, 1995

A humid, monsoon-cloud-topped June afternoon in Bangalore, India, was coming to a majestic close. It was the finals of the annual rolling shield cricket competition final between St. George's Public School and St. George's Private School, played at Webb's Ground. As is typical in India, the rich get richer, and the poor get poorer. Yet they often live side by side. This gulf is strikingly evident in the major cities and could easily be seen on the cricket field on that day.

The St. George's Private School students were affluent, whose parents were from the higher socioeconomic strata of the Indian society. As for the public school, the students were from a lower socioeconomic group. The parents, teachers, and classmates of both schools were present to witness the final. The spectators were seated around the boundary ropes, the schoolkids in their respective uniforms, and the teachers in the shaded pavilion. It was a holiday for both schools to witness the match.

The private school batted first and put up an imposing total of 250 runs in 50 overs. The public school was chasing the runs and was badly placed at 151 runs for the loss of 6 wickets at one stage.

But they had recovered to 215 runs for the loss of 8 wickets thanks to the brilliance of a twelve-year-old called Amay Indulkar. Opening the batting, he had bravely scored 96 runs so far, and all hopes of winning relied upon him farming the strike from the remaining three tailenders and carrying his bat throughout the innings. His back-foot drives, a hallmark of a great batsman, was the hallmark of his innings.

There were 4 overs left in the day's play for the public school's batsmen to chase the remaining 35 runs. Kiran Mehta, the captain of the private school, bowled an expensive over and conceded 16 runs. The target was reduced to 19 runs of 18 legitimate deliveries left to be bowled in the match. Amay Indulkar brought up his deserved century during that over with a classic on-drive off mid on for 4 runs.

Amay Indulkar now was on strike on 112 runs. The momentum was with the public school.

Amay hailed from a poor family residing in a small unit in the slums of Madivala. His father was killed in a road traffic accident several years ago, and his mother died of tuberculosis even before he could remember her. He was raised by his grandmother. She worked as a cleaner for the rich elite of Bangalore's social circles.

The match was getting tight, the tension palpable, but the bowling was complacent by the bowlers of the private school. They had bowled poorly all day, and Amay had made the most of this by striking several boundaries. The private school vice captain, Akshay Singh, hatched a plan. Being the local school bully, he decided upon gamesmanship. He decided to bowl a short delivery that would hopefully injure Amay so that he would not be able to bat any further, thereby making it easy to take the remaining 2 wickets and win the match.

Akshay had accomplices in the crowd. His classmate Faustin Franco, an Anglo Indian student, had a mirror in his hands. The plan was to reflect the sunlight into the batsman's eyes as he batted, hopefully blinding him temporarily, thus allowing the bouncer to take full effect and injure Amay. This plan was hatched weeks ago for counteracting against good opposition batsmen. Now that the game was slipping away from his team, Akshay signaled to Faustin in the crowd to carry it out.

Faustin unleashed the mirror. His classmates were all in support of this plan and covered him so that the teachers could not see what was happening. The sun was setting in the opposite direction to the batsman's line of sight and perfect to get the reflection into Amay's eyes.

The private school had a coeducation system, and the girls in the audience were cheering their heroes as well. Preity Lahoria, aged fourteen and daughter of the mighty Bollywood film producer Kishore Lahoria, was actually supporting the opposite team, the public school. She liked the fighting spirit demonstrated by the young Indulkar in chasing these runs. She prayed for her hero to score those runs.

A flash caught her eye. It was the mirror that Faustin was testing out. She knew what this was turning out to be.

Preity broke into the crowd of a dozen strong adolescent schoolboys and pushed them aside and then walked up to Faustin and chided him for his cowardliness. "How could you do this?"

"We want the trophy, you stupid girl. Get out of my way." His friends blocked Preity's attempts of grasping the mirror out of Faustin's hands.

Preity tried to call for help. There was none to be found. The headmasters were at special enclosures in the main pavilion far away. The fast bowler, Akshay, had just started his run-up and was running in to bowl to Indulkar for the first ball of the final three overs.

There was only one thing left to do—warn the umpires. Preity ran onto the field. The crowd was aghast at seeing a spectator run onto the field of play. Akshay had reached the popping crease and bowled to Indulkar, who did not notice the unexpected entry of Preity onto the field. Faustin reflected the sunlight. Indulkar saw the flash in his eyes and did not have the time to ask the bowler to stop as Faustin had so perfectly timed it, and Akshay had already delivered the short-pitched ball.

It bounced, and its hard core struck Indulkar on the left temple. He fell on the ground, blood pouring out profusely from the wound on his head onto his shirt and the pitch. The match ground to an abrupt halt. Preity was the first to reach Indulkar. He was in agony from the blow. After having had a bandage, he was taken off the field, and the match resumed. There was no apology forthcoming from Akshay or his teammates.

Akshay easily claimed the final wicket of the tailender. The private school had won over the public school by 18 runs.

An hour later, the respective school principals presented the winner's trophy to the private school and the man of the match in absentia to Amay Indulkar. A jubilant Akshay lifted the trophy and celebrated with his friends the facile victory.

A limousine pulled up the front of the school. Preity had organized transport for the injured Indulkar to the hospital and even paid for his medical bills using her pocket money.

Two days later, the same limousine was parked outside the Madivala government housing. Preity, who had bribed the chauffer to silence, entered the surroundings of poverty and realized her luck at her own good fortune and upbringing. She found the little brick unit where Indulkar lived and paid him a visit. His head in a bandage, he looked well and vibrant. They bid each other good-bye. Preity scrawled on a piece of paper "112 runs unbeaten" and handed it over to Indulkar. Indulkar autographed his signature underneath it and handed it back to her.

They parted ways for the next fifteen years and were to later meet again, in 2010, in that epic first match of this present series at Lord's.

The police car pulled over to the Upton Park address in London. Inspector Davidson and Landon Beau knocked on the door, and a young tired-looking Amay Indulkar answered them.

They sat down in his little home. Amay had cooked *bondas* and offered them some to go with strong Indian coffee.

"We are thinking of getting you back to playing the game and to show the match fixers that we are not intimidated by their threats."

"Inspector, I do not want to play cricket ever again. First, I have to study for my MRCP-1 UK postgraduate medical exams in three months' time. As you know, we doctors from overseas countries are always in the backseat for jobs here in the UK. I have said all that I can to that kind lady policeman who took my statement two weeks ago. For now, I have nothing more to say."

"Amay, we can promise you police protection. It was so well documented in the media about the death threats to your family if you were not to go with the match fixers' intentions. But we have the match fixer in this country and can catch up with him soon. We cannot show them that we are afraid of them."

"There's the other problem of my batting form. I have lost my batting form. You don't want to see me score zero runs again at the Oval in two days' time, do you?"

"Come on, Amay, you may not realize, but your thoughts have a profound influence upon your actions. You are zero runs only if you think yourself that low. Didn't the great West Indian all-rounder, Sir Gary Sobers, once write that you are down only if you *think* you are?"

"No, I shall still not play the game anymore." Landon detected an emotional tone in his voice to reveal a very distressed young man.

"Amay, can I ask what is really the matter?"

Amay Indulkar replied, "Nothing, Inspector. My poverty, which I have inherited from birth, is my problem."

Amay began to cry profusely. Landon consoled him. How could such a champion batsman, who had only just scored a majestic century at Lord's a few days earlier, be reduced to this emotional wreck? It had to be the result of an interaction with a woman gone wrong.

Davidson asked, "We've all been there before. We all remember a girl who broke our heart. We're only human, and it's okay to be a bit gun-shy. Who is she?"

"Preity Lahoria."

"Preity? The daughter of the Bollywood kingpin Kishore Lahoria? How did the two of you get involved?"

"Well, Preity helped me when I was injured by a bowler as a kid." He revealed the scar across his left temple, gained on that fateful day at Bangalore in 1995. "After my century at Lord's, she approached me and told me that she loved me. But that her father had arranged her marriage to the same fast bowler who caused me this injury back then."

"Let me guess. Akshay Singh?" asked Landon Beau.

"How did you guess?" asked Indulkar.

"Easy. There's only one obnoxious, arrogant bowler who hasn't matured much in the mind in that Professionals XI team, and that's him," replied Landon.

"The match fixers approached me. They asked me to accept one million pounds for scoring zero runs in the next two matches. I earned 70,000 pounds from my Lord's batting performance. I can earn close to 100,000 pounds for my batting at the Oval and then Lord's again. But what I cannot understand is why threaten my family if I don't obey?" asked Indulkar.

"How did he approach you?" asked Davidson.

"He introduced himself as Adam, a Sarjah-based entrepreneur. He at first enticed me with simple questions, like the pitch and weather conditions. I thought I could trust him. Then he introduced his real intentions. I have no one in the world, besides a little brother in India who works in information technology. I could really use this money from cricket to help me come up in life," replied Indulkar.

"We have images of this Adam character. We can potentially approach him and ask him to back off—in a way, protect you," said Landon.

"No thanks, Inspector, I'd rather not play at all," replied Indulkar.

There was nothing they could do. Perhaps asking Preity to talk to him might help convince him to give the game an attempt. They bid him good-bye and left his home.

"It's time to beard the lion in his own den. Let's announce the squad to play at the Oval tomorrow and then attract the match fixer to us. Once done, we'll talk him out of his threats for poor Indulkar. As for his morale, we need Preity here soon. Only she can convince him to play the game again. How that happens is out of our control; her father will never let us near her. But there's nothing like a woman's energy to boost a man's morale," said Davidson as they drove back to headquarters.

Chapter 10

Amelia Kanowski

Amelia never expected that she would ever have to get involved with law enforcement agents in any way or form in her life. She felt uneasy to have a police car parked outside her house—what would the neighbors think? Inspector Davidson seemed courteous on the phone. He was to arrive in a couple of hours.

She thought to herself about how this freaking game, cricket, was ruining her life. First, she had the most boring evening on assignment covering it. Its glamour was not even a millionth of the Victoria's Secret fashion show that she had covered in Paris the next day. It was played by flannelled fools, now dressed in pajamas and what appeared to be a glorified version of baseball. She couldn't understand how such a boring game could attract sponsors worth billions of dollars. Tennis is glamorous, golf is elegant, and cricket is just—in a word—boring. And now, she had to give evidence for a photo she took by accident—only because a suspect appeared in it. She fumed, *"Zum teufel!"*

It was eight p.m. that night. Kanowski had completed the day at work, typing in her report from the Victoria's Secret fashion show.

Amelia wondered why this apparent bad luck was befalling her. She had only just covered a few moments of that match.

She was dressed in her work outfit, awaiting the inspectors to arrive. She heard a car pull outside her home. Two men disembarked.

Her keen eye for fashion caught this very good-looking young man approaching the door, walking alongside the senior detective. His short blond hair, his clean-cut, well-groomed manner, his confidence, and all communicated to her from his demeanor and body language as a confident male within a few minutes of his arrival. Amelia gasped at the silky smooth embodiment of Landon, and when she greeted them at her front door, her attention was preoccupied with this fine specimen of manliness. The visitors introduced themselves as Inspector Davidson and Landon Beau, which Amelia could barely listen to as she shook hands with Landon.

Amelia Kanowski, aged twenty-eight, was lonely. The men she knew were either too needy or lacked any basic concept of romance. Belonging to generation X, where the advances in information technology led to a generation of social dinosaurs in terms of men and the reason for the dying days of romance, meant that romance was a dying art. Could this man be different? Could he revive the dying art of romance? She secretly prayed so.

She offered the inspectors herbal green tea, which was her favorite drink. Inspector Davidson began, "Amelia, how much do you know about what's going on so far?"

She pondered the question and replied, "I was told that I had inadvertently photographed some evidence, which may be of value in this case of the murdered coach." She seemed so sincere.

"That's right, Amelia. You captured an image of a match fixer. He is extremely well-known in the bookmaker circles. He was seen standing next to Indulkar, the star batsman of the Amateurs XI team. We believe that he was the one Indulkar revealed to us that his life would be threatened if he spoke out about match fixing, which you may have read about in the newspapers. We know who he is, and we know where he presently is in the UK. Due to confidentiality reasons, we are unable to reveal his name to you. But thanks for the picture—it was a vital lead. Can I ask, was there anything else you saw around you when you took that picture?"

"Is that all you came for, Inspectors? Well, there was nothing else I saw that would be of any help. I saw an Indian girl crying, followed by two people that looked like bodyguards. But other than that, nothing else. But then, I'm not trained to see these things because I'm just a fashion photojournalist!" replied Amelia.

"We'll keep you informed of further developments. Please call us if you remember anything else from that day. For the moment, only the police secretaries, database, Landon, you, and I know that you took that photograph and that this meeting ever took place. Your chances of being contacted by the perpetrators seem remote."

Landon felt a lump in his throat to leave such a beautiful woman behind without the prospect of meeting her again. She had lovely eyes, soft skin, perfectly aligned teeth, luscious lips; Landon wanted to hold her hand and comfort her—

but resisted. Professionalism prevailed. But his heart said otherwise.

They left the house and walked toward their police car, surrounded by the warm midsummer breeze that silently blew through the oak leaves that lined the London streets. The moonlight and streetlights clad the two men as they closed the doors. Davidson began to start the car's engine.

"Please stop!" said Landon.

"I beg your pardon?" asked a surprised Davidson.

"That girl is lonely and scared. I can't leave here without checking if she's okay," said Landon.

"Are you out of your mind? We have to catch the first available flight tomorrow morning at six in the morning to reach Manchester City. We have to meet your contacts and recruit a fresh team. I have to coach them well enough so that they can put up a decent performance at the Oval in two days' time against real cricket professionals. Indulkar won't play anymore. And you want to get back into that house and sweet-talk to that lady? Why? We did not break any bad news to her. We only reiterated to her the facts of our case," replied Davidson.

"I'm not leaving until she is mentally at peace, feels safe, and is comfortable," retorted Landon.

"Landon! This is not on. We have work to do. We're policemen, not psychologists. The criminals are laughing at us and drifting farther and farther away. The crime is hardly solved. Well, if you feel so strongly to stay, stay then. I'm driving away in five minutes if you're not back by then," exclaimed an angry Davidson.

Landon left the car and walked back toward Amelia's house.

Amelia, in the meantime, felt very distressed at discovering that she could potentially be targeted by match fixers if they had somehow come to know that she took the photo of one of them. Her mind began imagining people watching her when she was working, walking down the park. Who were these people? By what bad fate did she have to get entangled with this stupid game?

Amelia heard her cat cry out in front of the living-room window. She opened the window and let the cat in. It seemed frightened as it hastily leapt into the safety of her home.

"What's the matter, Otto? Why are you scared today?" asked Amelia.

As if for reply, a large hand protruded from outside the window and grabbed her left wrist. Amelia was too shell-shocked to scream. As if things could not get any scarier, the being to whom that hand belonged to emerged into sight.

He looked hideous, as if out of a Frankenstein movie. He had a large brow; short, unbrushed hair; an unkempt appearance; stunk of rotten meat; wore a sheep farmer's large gray uniform; and his eyes were large and bloodshot. He tried to climb into the room, but the small size of the window meant that, in his carelessness, he bumped his head onto the windowsill. That helped him let go of his grasp of Amelia.

Amelia screamed and ran toward her iPhone to dial 999. Her fingers shook, and her heart rate raced with the surge of adrenaline. A visceral fear for her life at large seized her, and she began to picture the best times of her life, flashing before her eyes. She could not dial the number correctly in desperation and panic.

The attacker had climbed into the house by now. He was eight feet tall and had some sort of an electronic instrument buttoned to his waist. He pressed a button, and a cold electronic voice spoke, "The laptop—give it to me!"

Amelia screamed as loudly as she could as this evil apparition of flesh and bones took steps toward her.

Landon was at Amelia's front door and gave it a knock. "Amelia, it's me, Landon. Open up please." He was answered by the scream.

"Bob, get in here!" he shouted across the road. Davidson was grumpy and turned on his car stereo, windows rolled up, and waited impatiently, arms folded across his chest, staring toward the front of the road, head bent downward.

"No time to waste," said Landon, as he took out his pistol and shot the lock three times until it broke. He pushed open the door. The noise of the shots was unheard to Davidson.

Landon broke the front door and saw the attacker with a gleeful look on his face and large doughy hands making their way for Amelia's neck as she stood motionless, wide-eyed and frightened, with her back to the wall.

Landon pulled out a wooden chair and hurled it across the attacker's back. The chair broke into pieces, and the attacker did not feel a thing. The challenge of a fight made the attacker change targets and approach Landon instead.

Landon punched him in the face. The attacker's head barely tilted in the direction of the force and instead replied with a cheesy smile and a shake of his finger. Landon decided to kick him in the groin—and he did—but the attacker seemed not to feel a thing. Landon tried judo and sidestepped to pull the attacker across. Bad idea. The attacker grabbed Landon instead across the torso and hurled him toward Amelia's large television, shattering the screen into pieces and leaving cuts and bruises on Landon's face and arms.

Amelia witnessed the horror of this attack and ran toward Landon to pick him up. Landon beseeched her in a weakened voice, "Call Bob—he's outside—run!" Amelia left a bruised and bleeding Landon and rushed outside into the darkness to get Bob.

Bob was still in his car. He glanced across his watch and spoke to himself, "Your five minutes are up, Landon. You are impossible." He got out of his car and was surprised to see Amelia running between the streetlights toward his car. He drew his semiautomatic Walther P99 gun out of its harness.

Landon only hoped that this attacker would not kill him before Bob arrived. Landon saw Amelia's purse within his vicinity. He reached for it and appreciated just how full of things a woman's handbag could really be—a reflection of all their daily responsibilities. He turned it upside down. A bottle of capsicum spray fell out. The attacker was now within hand's reach of Landon. Landon sprayed the capsicum directly between the attacker's eyes. He laughed at it and began to eat the spray in the direction of its exit from the bottle, with his large tongue hanging out, and came close to Landon's outstretched hand, as if to eat the bottle out of his hands.

At this point, Bob and Amelia entered the room. "Hands up, you. Are you all right, Landon?" asked Bob. The attacker decided that he'd had enough and made his way out through the backdoor. Davidson decided against firing any shots in case it upset the tranquil inner-city London neighborhood and instead radioed his police colleagues. "Code 75 Ealing."

Landon managed to mutter, "He was alone . . ." before passing out in Amelia's arms.

Later that evening, three hours later, the helicopters failed to detect anyone leaving the house. Kanowski had called Graham, explaining the situation, and had been granted compassionate leave off work. Landon had a few CT scans at St. Bart's Hospital, and all that was detected was external bruising, thereby ruling out any internal hemorrhage. His x-rays ruled out fractures or dislocations.

Amelia requested the nursing staff to meet Landon after he had been sutured. Landon was in a hospital bed on ward 35 for overnight observation.

A nurse approached. "Ms. Kanowski, we are unable to permit you meeting your friend. It's outside visiting hours." Landon suddenly appeared behind the nurse, all dressed up, with a mild bloodstained bandage across his brow, and smiled at the nurse. The nurse tried to stop Landon, "Hey, you can't leave. Doctor said you ought to spend the night here!"

Landon replied, "Oh, has he? I'm feeling better already," as he smiled and walked hand in hand with Amelia into the starry London night.

Chapter 11

Emergency Meeting

A groggy-eyed Inspector Harrison appeared at 11:45 p.m. at the Enfield HQ. He was dressed in jeans and a T-shirt and looked haggard as if he had just awakened from yet another night of poor sleep. He was joined by his secretary, Julie, a sutured and bandaged Landon, Amelia, and Bob. The Code 75 team had failed to locate the attacker, who, in all likelihood, had escaped by means of a getaway vehicle.

"My friends, welcome Amelia. We have just had a fresh development to this case. It appears that you may have something pretty important in your laptop or in your brain, young lady. I wonder—did you take any more pictures from that cricket match that you covered?"

"No, I have this facility to download pictures directly into my e-mail and send it to my work e-mail and boss."

"Well, it appears that you may be quite important in this case. We know that you pictured the match fixer earlier. The break-in to your house tonight—someone may have found out about that picture you were having in your camera and may want to get rid of that picture. Given that it pictured Adam, I can't think of anyone else but Adam being behind this," said Inspector Harrison.

"I agree, Nigel, we must question Adam. I wonder if you could arrange to get him arrested and bring him in for questioning."

"On what charges, my dear friend? He wasn't the man that Amelia and Landon have identified as their attacker tonight," said Harrison.

Inspector Harrison's mobile phone rang, and he answered it. "Yes . . . Very well . . . Good work, Russ. See your report in the morning."

Inspector Harrison turned to the group. "Right again, Landon. So glad I convinced you to come back into the force. Yes, the DNA analysis left on the scene by the attacker's blood samples from the windowsill has identified him formally on our database as none other than Slocum."

The room replied in unison, "Slocum?"

Landon asked, "Now the question is, who is he working for this time and why?"

The meeting adjourned. Landon and Amelia looked into each other's eyes. He wasn't going to let this lovely lady spend the night alone. Her home was cordoned off by the police.

"Hey, come over to my place tonight."

She agreed. They left the room together. Later that night, they were in each other's arms in Landon's hotel room. "Oh, Landon, stay with me. I can't feel safe until that monster is destroyed."

Landon replied, "Baby, feel safe in my arms. Everything's going to be all right. We'll go to Manchester together tomorrow. There we shall meet the rest of my team."

An hour later, they lay together in bed. The moonlight struck a ray between the two halves of the curtain. Landon had the gorgeously shaped Amelia in his strong, muscular arms. Their fingers were clasped with each other. He felt her gentle, soft femininity, the warmth of her cuddle, her radiant eyes shining like the reflection of the moon upon the River Rhine. She felt his male energy reaching out to her heart as if she could hear his thoughts and feel his dreams. Their hearts beat in unison. It seemed the perfect synchronous moment of their lifetimes. Her hair over his face, Landon heard Amelia whisper into his ear, "Thank you for saving my life."

They kissed passionately as their nimble, tall bodies twined underneath the warm duvets in their air-conditioned room. In their private and uninterrupted embrace, they felt like one organism and shared their mutual love.

Chapter 12

Manchester

The BA 777 flight landed in Manchester City. In it were the team of three—Inspectors Davidson and Landon Beau, and Amelia Kanowski. Through the window, the typically rainy Manchester weather was in full view.

Bob noticed the holding of hands throughout the flight between Amelia and Landon. Amelia woke Landon up as they were to disembark.

"Ever been to Manchester before, darling?" he asked as he yawned and awoke from his catnap.

"Several times," she replied, "but never with such pleasant company." They exchanged a quick kiss and joined the inspectors outside.

They checked into the Ibis Hotel and then proceeded to meet their first contact—Paddy McNally.

Paddy was Irish and was Landon's former club cricket teammate. He presently worked as a dance instructor at Salsa Fusions in Bury, Greater Manchester. They entered his studio.

He had short red hair. A lot of framed pictures of himself receiving trophies all over the world in salsa competitions were hung on his walls. His very walk was like a dance. His flexible shoulders were very noticeable to the team when they met with him.

"I'll join your team. It's been a long while since I have played cricket."

"Watch this, Inspectors," said Landon, as he proceeded to ask Paddy who his favorite cricketer was.

"Oh—easy," he replied. The Latin music was beating away in the background of the studio. He shouted across the room to a 36-24-36, salsa-dancing beauty who had long black hair that went down to her waist and doe-shaped Spanish eyes. "Hey, Carmen! Switch off the music. Switch on my other music."

She sighed disapprovingly at him, walked across the room, and picked up the remote. The room was filled with hard-rock music, and one of the large mirrors of the dance tutoring hall inverted to reveal a large television screen behind them.

"Oh, 1999—the memories. There was—that awesome World Cup cricket final at London. It was so nice to see my favorite cricketer reaching the pinnacle of his career."

Carmen arrived with a fresh Dukes cricket ball and bat and handed it over to Paddy. "I'm trying hard to get him away from cricket. No net practice indoors—that's an *order*! Such an unromantic game," she said as she looked disapprovingly at him again.

Paddy teased her, "Carmen, you look cute when you are angry."

The lights in the hall were dimmed. Paddy, dressed in jeans and carrying a portable mike attached to his belt, as a dance instructor would, pressed a few buttons on it. An overhead projector whizzed to life. A life-size hologram appeared. Landon instantly recognized the cricketer in the hologram. It was none other than the great Australian spin-bowling genius, Shane Warne. The hologram began to start his run up and deliver the cricket ball, right arm over the wicket. Paddy picked up a cricket ball and, as he was left-handed, proceeded to bowl across the dance floor. He resembled a perfect match to the hologram.

The hologram then turned into a batsman with batting gear and helmet, and Paddy picked up the cricket bat and again proceeded to show the police how his batting style resembled the great man as well. He began to play his strokes to imaginary bowlers—playing the sweep, cover drive, cut shot, French cut, on drive, off drive, pull, and hook shots.

He proudly remarked to himself, "I predict Ireland will win the one-day match against England at next year's World Cup! We are capable of chasing anything—even three hundred runs! Every Irishman's dream! O'Brien is our finest batsman."

"And why not?" replied Landon wryly. "Didn't the Dutch beat England at Lord's in a 20/20 international under floodlights every day?"

"The walls, Paddy. The walls. I don't want any indentations made by that cricket ball!" shouted Carmen across the room.

"Yes, my pet—looking even sexier when you are angry" was his cheeky reply.

He then proceeded to bowl several variations of leg spins across the dance hall to Inspector Landon and Amelia.

He was instantly hired for the Amateurs XI.

The next port of call was to an electrician's store. Landon's friend, Ray Shade, was an off-spinner for club teams and now, after retirement, had claimed to have invented a new type of spin. He was bald and had a deep voice. "There are only eleven types of off-spin deliveries. Why can't there be more?" asked Ray.

Landon replied, "Aren't arm ball, Chinaman, doosra, flipper, googly, carrom ball, off break, shooter, skidder, slider, and top spinner enough to bamboozle batsmen if bowled with sufficient variations in line and length and mixed about?"

"Ahhh, but I'm evil! I have learnt to bowl a ball that lands into a batsman's blind spot!"

Meanwhile in London, Preity Lahoria's family was packing for a short trip to Bangalore for her engagement to Akshay. Preity was teary in her bedroom. Her mother approached her.

"*Beti*, why are you crying?"

"Mom, I know that Akshay Singh is rich and famous and is an Indian national team international cricket player, but I just feel he is a bit too arrogant."

"But, *beti*, he is so well educated. Same school as yours and has such a nice position in the cricket. He earns millions of dollars every year playing for India, the Indian 20/20 Leagues, and now, this series."

"No, Mom. I like Amay. He is so gentle and warm and friendly."

"*Beti*, don't say that. Your father has known Akshay's father since childhood. Amay has no proper job, no money, and comes from a poor family."

"Mom, you don't get it, do you?" shouted back Preity as she stormed out of the house. "I'm going for a walk, and I'll be back in an hour's time."

She was accompanied by her two bodyguards. She walked to her favorite spot in Regent's Park, overlooking the Thames. The bodyguards stood a distance away and allowed Preity her personal space.

She began to cry. She took her *salwar kameez*'s shawl and used it to wipe her tears. She was arranged to get engaged to Akshay but did not like the man. The Bollywood world had deep ties with the families of both parties. Several films were to be produced with their respective fathers as joint directors. This engagement was worth billions of Indian rupees of revenues from Bollywood movie sales, the world's largest film industry. But her heart was not in it.

She heard a soft sound of someone approaching her. It was a beautiful woman, dressed in a red skirt and pink sleeveless top and wore black trainers and had her hair tied backward in a ponytail. She approached a grieving Preity and sat beside her on the bench.

"Hi there, I'm Lucy. Nice to meet you. Why are you crying?"

The London summer sun, the chirping of the birds in the trees, the joggers and cyclists, and busy traffic noise were all a background feature on the arrival of this peaceful woman. Her voice was deep, like a tenor, her eyes blue.

"I am grieving as I am destined to get engaged to Akshay in India in three days . . . He's very famous but has no manners. I want someone who I can relate to."

"Who is this that you really love?" asked Lucy.

"Amay," she replied. "He too is a cricketer but cannot find a full-time job as a doctor in this very competitive job market. He therefore batted at that cricket match, to earn himself money, and he batted so well at Lord's, but the match fixers are threatening to kill him and his family if he doesn't comply with their requests to dismiss himself cheaply."

"You must do what your heart tells you to do," said Lucy. "You must refuse to get engaged to this Akshay."

"But Amay has nothing in the world. My family has everything, and Bollywood tabloids and magazines are already calling this the engagement of the year."

Lucy replied, "Call Amay and tell him to play the match at the Oval. It's okay, it's going to be all right. I'll take care of things."

"Who are you?" asked Preity.

"I am sort of a caretaker." She placed a piece of paper with Amay Indulkar's phone number on it. "Call him today, and tell him to play for your sake at the Oval." Lucy walked away and was soon lost in the bustle of the London crowd.

Landon had previously organized a big meeting at the Press Club nightclub for that night. This particular nightclub in Manchester is the one that stays open the longest into the night. It often attracts the rich and the famous.

"So who are we meeting again?" asked Davidson.

"Viv Rickards," said Landon, with his mischievous smile.

Davidson jumped off the seat of the car. "You don't mean the great, great man—Sir Isaac Vivian Alexander Richards, one of five Wisden's cricketers of the twentieth century, the finest batsman of the century after Bradman, the greatest of all West Indians, the greatest of the great? But he's nearing fifty years old!"

"No, Inspector, I meant Viv Rickards," corrected Landon. "Rickards, like his namesake is also a hard-hitting batsman ideally suited for number 3. He is African and from Zimbabwe. He has the voice of an angel and sings at the Press Club every evening."

Landon, Amelia, and Davidson met with the club's live singer. He was a humble man and spoke with grace. "I am so lucky to be alive. I am aged thirty, and the average life expectancy in Zimbabwe is twenty-eight years. I am so happy to be alive. HIV and AIDS haven't claimed me. Glory to God in the highest. I sing my songs in his honor. Cricket is only a part-time hobby of mine. But I'll be glad to play."

They heard Rickards sing his songs. He was particularly adept at singing Lionel Richie and Sir Elton John songs. In between singing, Rickards shared a drink with Landon. "Let me introduce you to my American friend. Meet Ice Cool."

"You mean the major league baseball player Ice Cool? The one who hit a thousand home runs last season but he got banned for a drinking-and-driving charge?"

"That's the one. But he's on probation now and scheduled to participate in *Dancing with the Stars* here in the UK. He can be useful in your cricket team."

"As a pinch hitter up the order?" asked Bob.

They soon met with this powerful six-and-a-half-foot African American man, who then asked, "What game is it that you play? Cricket? Whatsat?"

Landon replied, "I'll explain the rules later. It's just like baseball. You just have to use our cricket bats and hit the ball as hard as you can outside the ground. And yes, if the opposition players hit the ball in the air, you have to catch it with your hands, not gloves."

"Hey, why can't they make new rules and allow fielders to have gloves like we do in baseball?"

He allowed himself to try out this experimental game. Little did he know that he was the first-ever professional baseball player who was also going to play first-class cricket in history.

While they were having drinks, they did not notice an old man in his early eighties, probably a bit too old to be at a nightclub, in a black suit and black hat, watching them from the distance. Instead of a walking stick, he carried a shepherd's cane.

As Landon's group said their good-byes and walked outside, this man proceeded to follow them out.

"Damn Manchester—roads blocked and rain, rain, rain," said Davidson. He proceeded to take a narrow alleyway. Hopefully, it would lead to Mancunian Way and, with that, to their hotel. The road was cobblestoned and freshly drenched in rain. Davidson had the car's wipers in full swing. The rain was pouring hard. The car lights were flashed ahead, and as they reached the end of the narrow alleyway road, they were greeted by two canes crossed against each other and a piece of paper tied with a string, hanging from the end of one of the canes. The car came to an abrupt halt. Amelia squeezed Landon's hand in the backseat, and he drew his firearm, ready for any unexpected attacks.

Landon and Davidson reached out for their guns. Davidson stepped outside the car, checked the surrounding area, and approached the blockade. Two shepherd's wooden staffs crossed and the letter. Davidson untied the letter; he felt his heart leap in excitement. It read,

Egerton Crescent

2200 hours

—Shepherd's Triad

Back in London, Preity stood by an outside phone booth and dialed Indulkar's number. Indulkar answered from work.

"Amay, I just need to tell you one thing. Please play for me one last time. I love your batting. For my sake. At the second match at the Oval Cricket Ground. Please, Amay."

Chapter 13

Face to Face with Adam the Match Fixer

Inspector Davidson drove past the famous Manchester Cathedral, the John Rylands Library, and entered Whittington.

They approached Egerton Crescent Street. They disembarked. There was a solitary person walking across to the homes that lined the streets. They waited—2230 hours. No one about.

Then an old man with a black suit and hat approached the group. He was walking on a shepherd's cane. Landon shouted across the street, "Who are you? We're meaning no harm. You asked us to meet you here."

The man stopped. He stood more erect than would be expected for an octogenarian. He pulled off a plastic mask covering his face to reveal a much younger man in his forties. He introduced himself as Jim Ayres of the Shepherd's Triad.

"We are the police. But can I ask why all this fuss?"

Jim replied. "This is just to warn you that—she is on her way."

"Who is she?" asked Landon

"You'll find out soon enough. She's already here and will soon be meeting you."

"Is that good or bad?" asked Landon.

"Both—I was referring to two women. One very good, one very evil. The bad one came first. And the good one has now come to negate the very bad one. The good one will soon be calling on the youngest of you all—Landon. The bad one has already hired someone very strong to kill. And he kills for pleasure."

"Can you tell us more?"

"That money man is in the restaurants across the road. He cannot be trusted."

"You mean the match fixer?"

"Yes, I was referring to Adam. He just met with the two detectives. Obviously, they didn't get much out of him."

"Did you want to tell us more?"

"I realize that you are police officers. I'm just giving you news that the good woman has arrived. She very rarely arrives. And she is a friend. Plus, I also know that Graeme Dawson is actually alive. Machines are keeping him alive in London."

"One last thing: you ought to meet Orson Dawson and book yourself on the first available flight to India. Preity's engagement is supposed to happen there in about twenty-four hours after conclusion of the Oval match. In fact, the postmatch celebrations are to take place in Orson's private A380. Then the engagement in India at a South Indian Hill station luxury resort, then they fly back to London for the third and final match two days later."

"Why are you telling us all this?"

"Just listen to me. I cannot tell you more. My life may be put in danger. The bad people are after me too. I'll call you in two days' time. Trust me. The person you'll need to call in India is called a Mr. Byragi. He lives at Coorg. He'll provide you with a vital piece of information that you should use to find the Enchanted Willow. Graeme was after this bat. He wanted to get rid of the evil around the team. It's much more than match fixing. That's all I can tell you."

"Where is this Enchanted Willow? Does it even exist?"

"It can only be found if you trace it by its history. It will give Amay Indulkar his batting form and confidence back, and he can win you the series."

With that, he disappeared into the darkness of the South Manchester alleyways.

"I'll be damned. I'll order his arrest straightaway for withholding information or obstructing the course of justice. Who does he think he is? He could be a hoax. The Shepherd's Triad is nothing but a story," growled Davidson.

Landon replied, "Wait a second, he may be right. He did after all know the meeting between the private detectives and Adam and that Graeme was alive. He did say that he would get in touch with us soon. All supposedly confidential information. He might be useful with more information later. I understand your point, Bob, that he is technically a suspect, as an e-mail before Graeme's attack was addressed to him, but for now, I'd let him go, and I'd monitor events of the next few days to see if they come true as he said so that we can question him later, if need be."

"Who were those women he was referring to?" asked Davidson.

"I don't know, but I guess we'll find out soon, like he said we would," said Landon. "But at least we now have most of our Amateurs XI Cricket Team in place. Add Chris Dawson and the Canadian Milton Keans, who stayed behind from the original squad, and we have ten players, including me and yourself, Bob. All we need now is a wicket-keeper."

They started to drive back into Manchester City to meet the private detectives. They entered Rusholme, parking besides the Gulabi Hotel. The Curry Mile is the longest group of restaurants in Manchester. Located at Rusholme, along Wilmslow Road, it contains over one hundred individual restaurants. Despite it being 11:30 p.m., the whole street appeared alive and vibrant. They saw three Subcontinental men across at the far end. There was loud *bhangara* music to be heard coming from the restaurant, whose beats matched the sounds of Landon's footsteps along the rain drenched footpath of Wilmslow Road.

The largest of the three stood up as he saw who was approaching and spoke to his two guests in perfect *Urdu*, "Excuse me, *bhais* [brothers], *shukriya* [thank you] for the kebabs and lamb *karahi*. I need to talk to these two gentlemen."

He had a pot belly, a French beard, and carried two mobile phones. He was dressed in a casual white T-shirt and blue jeans. He was Adam, the chief bookie from the match fixers.

Landon and Bob approached Adam, while Amelia stayed behind in the car. Adam said, "Let's go inside my quarters."

"No, let's talk outside. We have a lot to talk about," said Landon with a steely look in his eyes, looking at the most obvious suspect of the Dawson murder case.

They sat on one of the restaurant chairs, and Adam ordered three glasses of mango lassi.

"What do you two want?" asked Adam.

"Adam, we need you to stop this game of match fixing. We need to have a fair game of cricket. And why do you threaten the life of innocent Amay Indulkar?"

"I have withdrawn all offers of money to that boy. I did not realize he had such a hard upbringing in India. I thought that he was one of those spoilt rich T20 kids," said Adam.

"Adam, why fix matches at all? The public have lost confidence," asked Davidson.

Adam nonchalantly replied, "How much do you know about us? I have bosses too, you know. I am just a middleman. The Mafia of the Mumbai underworld are not a wise thing to make angry. They can chop your bodies to a million pieces, like they did last year to some weak bookmaker who thought he could flee from India to South Africa. They caught him and did all that to him."

Adam added, "Cricket is no longer controlled by England. India now controls 60 percent of cricket's revenue. And cricket's headquarters has shifted from London to Dubai now. There was a time that the imperial powers had double-voting rights and we Subcontinentals were oppressed. Now we financially rule the game. We do business the way it was always done in the subcontinent. We only want a small piece of the billions from this new 20/20 cricket—just a few millions, really."

Adam continued, "As for the match fixing, all we are doing is a little harmless betting. Like you would do at the races. Over number 12.3 will be a no-ball deliberately bowled by the bowler paid by us to bowl a no-ball—and there you have it. Only one run conceded. The interest in the game will be so much more."

Adam then explained the specifics of match fixing. "We can even take bets barely ten seconds before a fixed event. It's that narrow a time gap. There are several dollars involved in illegal match fixing. In legal betting, a company could make 40 million pounds for one match. Whereas in illegal betting, for a match of high interest, in one city alone, 200 million dollars could be generated. In total, one billion dollars could be generated per match. Annually, that would turn out to be 50 billion dollars—in illegal betting. We are worth a lot, lot more than Dawson's three-match series. We make his few millions look like waiter's change in front of our money."

Landon interrupted, "Adam, do I have it clearly stated by you that Indulkar's offer to throw away a match is dropped?"

Adam replied, "Yes. But that's because my bosses have been kind to the young boy. They might give me fresh orders soon, and I may have to bribe players again, including the boy. The Professionals XI is controlled by the ICC. They are real international cricketers. The Amateurs XI, I can deal with more easily. No such control on them from the ICC, you see. They are easy pickings."

Davidson asked, "Adam, two more things. Let's start with the deceased coach, Graeme Dawson. What did the two of you talk about in his room? And did you kill him?"

Adam replied, *"Arre oh* [good heavens], so I am a murderer now? I met that coach because he wanted to tell me to stop bothering Amay. I told him that I had orders from the subcontinent from my bosses. He just didn't get it. So I left in a huff. I swear on my mother that I did not kill him. In any case, my bosses have been merciful and have decided to let Amay off so that he can play his cricket again. Be sure to tell him this good news."

Davidson asked, "And lastly, Adam. This man work for you—an eight-foot-tall South Island, New Zealand, contract killer called Slocum, who strangles people with his bare hands? I had a run-in with him last night. We know that he was with you at the hotel room during the night of Graeme Dawson's murder."

"No, he's not one of mine. But look who's being untruthful now? I know that the coach is actually alive in a hospital. You can't expect me to be sincere if you police people are not sincere yourselves! I have to follow my orders. But for now, as of this moment, my bosses have not given me any fresh orders. So no one will get bribed to underperform," replied Adam.

"What about tomorrow?" Landon asked.

Adam replied, "Tomorrow is a different day. Things change." And with that, he burst into self-applauding laughter by himself.

At this point, an irked Landon breathed in deeply, his shoulder muscles tensing, with his inner bowels twisting at the arrogance of this match fixer, and declared firmly, "We can arrest you for being an accessory to murder, withholding information, plotting to bribe. Why should we not arrest you? We have video footage of you entering and leaving the coach's room at the time of the murder and finding the coach alive before you saw him and dead after you left the room!"

Adam laughed. "Son, you don't know how powerful my bosses are. They are being merciful this time. Maybe not some other time. You better go back to your regular life in Wigan, in your old job, and don't get involved with me. I know a lot of things. I know that Graeme is alive. I know whom you wrestled with last night. I know whom you met at Egerton Crescent an hour ago. I know everything. We have contacts everywhere. Ha ha ha ha ha!"

He turned toward Landon and brought his face closer to Landon's, staring into it in a confronting manner, and said in a dark tone of voice, "I also know about that wife of yours—Sabrina. Too bad, my condolences, we didn't have anything to do about it. How were we to know that you chose to ignore her complaints of headaches that morning because you were too busy pursuing us in Leeds in 2000 and doing your job like a public-servant lapdog and told her she had a case of 'hormones,' when she ended up having that fatal miscarriage?"

Landon felt his anger boil over at those words. He reached across the table and grabbed Adam by the shirt, spilling lassi all over Adam's trousers. Adam's two iPhones fell to the ground, and he exclaimed, "One thousand pounds for my iPhones, twenty pounds for the laundry, you police bastards will have to cough it up! I'm talking to my solicitor!" Inspector Davidson intervened and separated the two before they could get involved in a punch-up.

"That's not what happened to Sabrina. It proves that you people do not really know each and every thing. She died of a rare complication of a normal pregnancy. I am quite sensitive about certain things, yes," growled back Landon, breathing heavily like an animal at war. Adrenaline was surging through his belly, his body posture pugilistic and combative, only held back by a pacifying Davidson.

"Is that why you are alone and lonely? Guilt?" asked a cocky Adam.

They almost got into fisticuffs again. Inspector Davidson and the hotel staff again had to intervene. The *bhangara* music continued to play.

Adam shamelessly continued the taunting, "Oh, I see! Someone is 'sensitive about certain things.' You see, we know everything. I suggest you calm down. I know your date of birth, your social security number, your passport number, your blood group, the type of police gun in your pocket, your Gmail passwords—and a lot more. We bookies are very well-informed. There is so much about us that you don't know about—let's keep it that way. We probably know more about you than you know about yourself. And we are very dangerous to cross."

Landon and Bob felt powerless at this wealth of confidential information that his bookmaker possessed.

Adam carried on, "So if you really want to arrest me, they'll just send another one in my place. More powerful and, hopefully, nastier. Maybe more than one person. I could actually help you. Perhaps—if you do one or two spot fixing at certain moments in the match I tell you to do, we can call it even."

"No, Adam. I will not be part of this plot. Thanks for the offer," said Landon

Adam replied, "You know, detectives, there is one thing I do not understand. This perplexes me. There seems to be someone else involved in this 'murder'—not just me. I don't know, I may be wrong, but there is someone more dangerous than me involved in all this. Whom, I don't know. I know you people cannot trust a word I say because I am basically a money-worshipping sinner. But hear me for once. I did not kill the coach, and I did not want to steal your girlfriend's laptop last night. I don't know who did."

Adam continued, "Besides, cricket has never been as interesting as it is now. The eyes of the world are watching every ball in this short series. A total of one-and-a-half billion television viewers from across the globe would be watching. So much money at stake—350 billion dollars! Such a grand experiment carried out in such a large scale, and I control this game! Ha ha ha ha ha!"

Adam was lost in self-amusement. "For a game supposedly displaying so much of psychology and being unromantic to women, it has done very well. We really have a thriller here— not just the matches, also the juice of whodunit to the coach and our subcontinental spice of match fixing added to the *biryani* of this contest. *Wah reh wah!*"

Adam concluded, "In the end, I would like to know who really tried to kill Graeme. That's your job, Inspectors. Ha ha! Lucky you. Lastly, I would not bother with those Shepherds— just a set of peaceful old men, who think they look after the game. Ha! We have slain them before like helpless sheep, and we'll not hesitate to do it again. I've met Byragi in India before—nice chap. You'll meet him soon. Give him my regards."

They did not shake hands and parted. Adam rejoined his shady friends in the corner.

Landon phoned Amay to inform him that the match fixers have verbally decided to withdraw their offer of money to underperform. Amay agreed to play again. Amay sent an e-mail to Preity, informing her of this decision.

They caught the first flight back to London the next morning, joined by Ice Cool, Viv Rickards, Paddy McNally, and Ray Shade.

Chapter 14

Net Practice

Landon led the meeting at the Enfield HQ. He was in the company of Bob Davidson, Harrison, Amelia, and Julie, as well as the new additions to the team—Ice Cool, Vivian Rickards, Paddy McNally, and Ray Shade. He introduced the new team members to the three cricketers who stayed behind from the original Amateurs XI team—Milton Keans, Dean Delaney, and Chris Dawson. Landon began, "Let's put the cards on the table. We have this sort of a line up:

1. Opener: Amay Indulkar is our obvious choice (India).
2. Other opener: will be me, Landon Beau. I'll also bowl medium pace. I am also the captain of the team (England).
3. Number 3 batsman: Ice Cool. Role is as a pinch-hitter for quick runs (USA).
4. Number 4 batsman: Dean Delaney, to steady the innings (Australia).

5. Number 5 batsman: Vivian Rickards, grafter type of batsman, to anchor the innings (Zimbabwe).
6. Number 6 batsman: Bob Davidson, to shore the tailenders. Vice captain of the team (England).
7. Number 7 batsman: Vacant. We need a wicket-keeper.
8. Number 8 batsman: Paddy McNally, bowling all-rounder. Left-arm leg spin (Ireland).
9. Number 9 batsman: Chris Dawson, bowling all-rounder (England).
10. Number 10 batsman: Ray Shade, right-arm off break bowler (England).
11. Number 11 batsman: Milton Keans, right-arm fast bowler (Canada).

"We don't have a substitute fieldsman. We probably may not need one. We are only playing two 20/20 games—the need for one appears less likely. Bit of a gamble. But before all that, let's find a wicket-keeper."

Harrison announced, "Very, very well done, team. You have all achieved greatness in adversity. You have cleared up so much of the problems we faced forty-eight hours ago. Now go have some fun and practice. The match at the Oval starts tomorrow by 2:00 p.m. Landon and I are going for a scouting session to find a wicket-keeper."

The team entered the other major cricket ground besides Lord's, in London, namely, the Brit Oval, colloquially known as the Oval. Perched in the center of the city and pictured on the characteristic gigantic metallic frame of the gas station in the background, it was the venue for the second match of the series.

Landon and Harrison walked along Leicester Square. Landon began, "Inspector, there's this Slocum matter. The match fixers, and even I, believe that we may be dealing with a third party here. And a very well-informed one. Who this party is, I do not know.

"How is Fartington? I haven't heard anything about her, so far."

"Cindy's very malicious and a backstabber who is well-known in the business circles for her malicious acts. But I can't imagine why she would want to cross a boss she has been working for for the past twenty-five years. She really is a shrew."

"Why do you say malicious?"

"She's nicknamed in London business circles as the Black Widow. She is known to sexually seduce businessmen and turn them over to favor business deals for Hedwig. Hedwig denies all of this, of course. She once complained about one of my detectives for saving her life when her luxury ocean liner sank on holiday off Battersea. My team saved her life. The complaint and subsequent lawsuit was about her broken manicured nail. She took out 20,000 pounds off our department as compensation. The obnoxious little weed!"

They passed a park in Chinatown. A large crowd of Chinese university students were cheering the person in the middle. "Let's see what this is all about," said Landon.

They approached the group. They seemed to be playing a game of soccer. Only that they were taking turns striking the ball into the goal, kept by an athletic Chinese man. He seemed to block every single goal kicked at him by the students. They cheered each and every goal saved.

Landon's face lit up. Harrison moaned, "Landon, I don't like it when you have that look in your eyes. Another brilliant idea, perhaps?"

"Quick, let's contact Julie at HQ. I think I know who that person is." He clicked a photograph of the goalkeeper and picture-messaged it to Julie. Julie replied soon enough, confirming the identity of the person to be Ling Zhang-Hue, the present Chinese national football team goalkeeper, on a holiday to England. More importantly, he was banned for a month, for frivolous disciplinary reasons, by the soccer board of his home country and currently available to play any other sport.

Landon proudly exclaimed, "Inspector, I think that we have just found ourselves the final missing link in our team— our wicket-keeper!"

At the break, Ling Zhang-Hue was being swamped for autographs.

"*Qing qianming* [autograph please]," requested Harrison. Ling looked up to the two Caucasian detectives, surprised at their command of Mandarin. "Relax," said Harrison, "these iPhones have translator applications. Would you like to make some money and gain fame and play a different kind of sport at the same time?"

"What kind of sport?" asked the young Chinese man.

"You just have to keep doing what you are doing, but the ball is much smaller, can travel a little faster, you have better gloves to catch the ball—I'll explain. Let's talk somewhere else," replied Harrison. After signing all the autographs, the trio headed back toward the Oval.

The net practice session was in full swing. The automatic-pace bowling machine was firing the ball around eighty to ninety miles per hour. Landon, Indulkar, Delaney, and McNally were all batting well in the nets.

The bowlers found a rhythm. Keans and Dawson bowled good lines and lengths and were able to make the ball swing. Shade practiced his off-spinners on the batsmen.

Rickards sang cricket songs to boost the morale. He sang the 1970s Australian World Series Cricket song, "C'mon Aussie C'mon," and the great West Indian cricket calypso hymn, composed by Lord Beginner after the 1950 Lord's Test match, "Cricket Lovely Cricket."

Ice Cool was able to strike the ball well, using horizontal batting strokes as in baseball. "Hey, man, you English guys sure have a nice game goin'. Us Yanks could take this game up sometime. I kinda like hitting the ball out of the park and scoring them home runs. So cool!" he drawled in his American accent.

Harrison said, "Let him think it's that easy. In reality, it's not. He could score some vital 'home runs' for us and hit a few sixes and fours in the process before eventually getting caught out. He is obviously the X factor, the surprise element in our batting line-up. His technique may not be so sound, but that's okay. In 20/20 cricket, it's all about getting the runs quickly, not how you get them that matters. After all, even the great Sir Geoffrey Boycott of England once stated that 20/20 cricket is a form of baseball—it's about how far you can hit it. I couldn't agree more with that wise man's assessment of this abbreviated version of our sport. Before the opposition bowlers work out his technique, it would be too late in the series, as it's only two matches. For now, let him enjoy the game."

Davidson said, "They seem to be picking up the game well now and seem to be able to understand how it's played. Takes me back to my childhood days when I first discovered cricket. We had such fun explaining the game, especially to the non-cricket-playing countries."

They explained the wicket-keeping basics to Zhang-Hue, and he was soon able to leap across the stumps and take catches and saves and learned how to stump batsmen out. He particularly liked diving across and taking catches behind the stumps, like he would do as a goalkeeper in soccer. He also seemed keen to bat.

"Things are going our way at last!" said Harrison later that evening as he poured champagne into his glass at the change rooms. He finally looked like he was catching up on some sleep and allowed himself a chuckle for the first time in days. "I can finally enjoy a glass of champagne. I only wish that we catch the coach's murderer, put up a decent show at these last two games, and find the poison that kept Graeme in suspended animation—if only life was that simple."

Landon also commented with "We have broken up a complex puzzle into simple pieces. We have had unexpected developments and took them by the collar. We have used every lead we could get. We deserve a few good results."

At this point, they left for a nearby restaurant for a well-deserved meal with the full team.

Chapter 15

The Oval Match

The sky was gun-barrel gray, overcast, and the ground damp—a typical first half of the English summer weather, when the ball swings and seams around. The pitch had very little grass on it and easily buckled in under the key test.

Perfect bowling conditions.

Captains Landon and Akshay went in for the toss for the second of three matches of this series. Akshay won the toss and elected to field. The large crowd on the ground—whose appetite had been whetted by the media reports of match fixing, of new players in the team, and the ongoing experiment of who can play better 20/20, the game's shortest format—had come to have their questions answered. The questions on most people's minds and lips were, "Are amateurs as good as professionals? Was it really easy for anyone and everyone to play 20/20, or does it require skill at the professional level, like one-day and Test cricket?"

Chinese cricket officials were at the game to watch Ling Zhang-Hue play his first game. He was creating history as the first-ever Chinese player to play international cricket since the West Indies off-spinner Ellis Achong, nearly seven decades before.

The batsmen, unfortunately, found the going too tough. Landon Beau crashed the second delivery he faced for a crisp cover drive for four runs, but then the extra swing on the ball took an outside edge, and he was caught behind. Out for four runs. Score four runs for one wicket.

Akshay began to taunt Indulkar. "So you are a glutton for punishment? I hit you in Bangalore, and you still have no shame. That helmet of yours can listen to my iPod music." He trundled in, dug the ball in short, and Indulkar ducked to get the ball past.

"Still standing? I want to wipe you from the face of the earth," muttered Akshay. Next ball, similarly short, struck Indulkar on the left elbow.

"I'm going to murder you!" he said as he bowled a yorker with a vicious inswing that forced Indulkar to lose his balance and that crashed into Indulkar's leg stump, and he was out for a duck.

As if this wasn't enough, Akshay taunted him again on the way back. "You can't do anything right with the bat, you fluke. I'll get you at Lord's for a duck again. Congratulations on scoring three ducks in a row. Ha ha haw haw haww!"

Score: four runs for 2 wickets at the end of 2 overs.

Enter Ice Cool. The Professionals XI bowlers were taken aback at his horizontal bat stance from his American baseball background. He proceeded to club 4 huge sixes of the next 6 deliveries, only missing 2 of them. "What an easy-peasy game," he remarked.

Score 28 runs for 2 wickets.

Batting at the other end was Dean Delaney.

Harrison at the dressing room gasped, "Well, now we have some action!"

After 6 overs, the Amateurs were well placed at 50 for 2. But Ice Cool eventually holed out to the spin bowlers and was dismissed for 36 runs.

Bob Davidson and Delaney built the innings, but they were soon nearing the completion of their 20 overs. Dawson and McNally went for some big hits, but their eventual score of 156 for 8 after 20 overs, though respectable, was hardly enough to challenge the Professional unit.

The professionals had good batting conditions as the clouds gave way by midday, and the overhead afternoon sun had dried the pitch's moisture. They scored the 157 runs for a small cost of 3 wickets by the twelfth over.

The fielding of the Amateurs XI was good, and the diving catch taken by Ling and the tight line and length and variations in the air from Ray Shade's off spin were the only positives to come out of it.

The three-match series was now level at 1-1, with all to play for at Lord's.

Landon felt dejected. He hated losing. He was surprised that Hedwig Dawson was actually satisfied with the overall performance of his team despite their loss.

Dawson, in a live interview that evening, said that he was pleased how a new team with no coach and a couple of noncricketers actually made it look respectable. He was actually smiling on camera for the first time in his public life.

Landon wasn't. A defeat is a defeat. Amelia tried to console him, but he was just too tired to take it on board. He said, "I need to be alone for a while." He excused himself and walked along Great George Street toward the Waterford Bridge.

He was exhausted. He was trying to solve an attempted murder mystery, had fought a goliath of a villain who was still at large, recruited and trained a new cricket team, played and captained a 20/20 match that had just been lost, answered the media, travelled to Manchester for a day, met unknown people there, clashed with match fixers—he clearly needed a break.

He walked past the Partridge Pub. It was seven in the evening, and as the late summer sunset had engulfed London in its entire glow, he made his way to the Waterford Bridge that overlooked the River Thames. He turned on his iPhone to listen to Bryan Adams's song "Heaven." He found that particular song consoling in times of distress. He also felt that he needed to catch up on his sleep.

He did not notice a lady approach from his right side. She was dressed in a jogger's tracksuit outfit, dark sunglasses, and had earphones on, listening to music playing through her iPod, and had her hair in a ponytail.

"Nice view, isn't it?" she chirpily quipped.

"Sort of—depending if you are referring to the sun's setting rays or to me?" replied Landon.

She laughed. She found this intelligent, charming young man attractive and took a few steps toward him. "Hi, I'm Lucy. I'm pleased to meet you." She took off her sunglasses to reveal her blue eyes.

Landon was exhausted at this point. "If you would excuse me, I'm fairly exhausted at the moment. I'm not feeling terribly social. Not in the mood for an autograph."

This kind lady seemed to listen to him. "It's okay, okay, Landon. Everything's going to be all right."

Landon Beau was stunned. "How did you know my name was Landon?"

"You look like a Landon—you are tall, athletic, fast moving, and intelligent, strong, funny, charming—a knight in shining armor."

"Flattery will get you anywhere," quipped Landon. He felt that there was nothing to lose. He could do with a few minutes of expression of his frustrations to a stranger. He'd feel a bit better, and it would also probably make her leave in ten minutes.

"I saw you captain your team today. You were very honorable as a leader," said Lucy.

"Do you want an autograph then?" asked Landon

"No, Landon, I have good news for you. Your life is about to change dramatically," said Lucy.

"What do you mean? You don't know me. I agree the tabloid newspapers do write some personal stuff about sportsmen, but we are essentially strangers."

Landon was going to ask her to leave. It was making him feel a bit uneasy.

"I know you met with a friend of mine two nights ago in Manchester. Jim—rings a bell?"

Landon was astonished to hear this. How could she have known of such a meeting?

"I was the good lady Jim was referring to. The friend. I am here to help," said Lucy.

Landon decided to listen.

"Your team can win the final match. What's keeping the real wrongdoers from getting caught is if your Amateurs XI team loses—Dawson loses lots of money from this costly cricket experiment of his, and the culprits get away scot-free. I was there in the hotel room when Graeme was put to sleep—"

Landon interrupted, "Wait a minute, all this is classified information. How did you get to know of all of this?"

She replied, "I just do. Only you can do it, Landon. The wrongdoers are close by. You have actually already met with them. All you need to do now is to think and act, and time will reveal the real perpetrator. But for your team to win, you need to recover the Enchanted Willow."

"Enchanted Willow! But it's an artifact and an old wives' tale—essentially a fairytale. It doesn't actually exist! And even if it does, as in Orson's museum, it doesn't work the way it should."

"Yes, it does," she replied. "My university background is medieval history. The object within the bat can be traced back to the middle ages. It was a sacred object called Penta, with special powers. It is hidden within the top half of the bat. Now you must make haste and set for India on Orson's private jumbo jet. He is hosting today's postmatch party on his plane, and they are all attending Preity and Akshay's engagement party tomorrow in India. You should be there to meet another friend who will contact you. His name is Byragi."

"What if I don't?" asked Landon.

Lucy replied, "Cricket will die. The match fixers will continue to make it look as if all games are fixed. A cheapened and easy version of the game, like 20/20, will look unplayable for non-cricket-playing countries to adopt and will look difficult for kids to take up. Thus, Test cricket and one-day cricket, which are already slowly being played less, will get even lesser. Fewer countries will adopt cricket—the game won't spread. The public will lose interest. Other sports, like soccer, will rule the world of sport."

She continued, "Most importantly, you will never catch the real criminal if you don't get on that plane to India. The big clue will be revealed there. Byragi will show it to you."

"Anything more you wish to say?" asked Landon. "Tell me you aren't some deranged fan stalking me!"

Lucy ignored the remark and continued. "Yes, your batting form. I think that you need to use the most potent inspirational force in the world to get you your form back," said Lucy, respectfully, despite Landon's growing impatience.

This woman off the street could read his mind.

"Who did you say you really are?" asked Landon curiously.

"A medieval history student. But that's not important. I was referring to *love*," said Lucy.

"What's love got to do with it?" asked Landon.

"A lot!" said Lucy. "I'm sure you have feelings for her."

"Who?" asked Landon.

"Sabrina," replied Lucy. "You see, Landon, let me give you a quick lesson on love. 'Love is patient, love is kind. Love does not boast, it is not rude. It is not self-seeking, it is not easily angered. It keeps no record of wrongs. It rejoices in the truth. It always protects, always trusts, always hopes, and always perseveres.'"

Landon listened with interest. Lucy continued, "What's gone wrong in today's society is the lack of love. The above words were taken from the Bible. God is love. Love conquers all. It's the only way two people can find any happiness in the world.

"People's lifestyles are busy these days. Quick thrills out of lust to satisfy one's physical needs are preferred by many who are not aware of the true concept of love. Such liaisons only end in the trash heap of broken relationships that we see around us.

"We humans have the highest brain-to-body-weight ratio of any other species on the planet, and medical science only knows 1 percent of how much the brain works. So that means, much of the brain's function is a mystery. We all have to die one day, and those of us who have not sinned will go to heaven. There, we will all be happy together. In heaven, we are at a higher level of our consciousness. There is no lust or physical distraction in heaven—only pure love. Sabrina, you, Amelia, and I, and those who rejected lust and embraced true love on earth. Our brains, in a higher state of function in heaven, will find true love by connecting with each other alone, rather than by physical needs. This is why it's important to have love on earth. Even to show love towards your enemy—forgiving and forgetting what they have done to you.

"You loved Sabrina. But Amelia loves you too. I appeal to you to allow the love between Amelia and yourself to grow. That energy will drive you towards solving the crime and beating the Professionals XI.

"I'm afraid I can't stay any longer than this. It's getting dark, and my cats need to be fed now. I'll call you in two days' time, after you return from India," said Lucy in farewell.

Landon watched her disappear into the distance as she jogged away. He wondered, *Who is this mysterious person?* He was so amazed at her knowledge of the case that he didn't even find the time to capture an image of her on his iPhone for Julie to verify or even call for backup from the police. If a stranger off the street knew of this murder investigation so intimately, who else knew? If the Shepherd's Triad were weird enough, now it appears he had an enamored fan.

As if to bring him back to reality, his iPhone rang. It was Inspector Davidson. "Have you packed just yet? Amelia is all packed up. So are we. Orson Dawson's private A380 jets off from Gatwick in two hours' time. You know how congested the Friday evening London Underground and traffic are like."

He turned and made his way back to the Oval.

Chapter 16

Orson Dawson

A large A380 at Gatwick Airport was preparing for departure. It had personalized identification markings—a gigantic alphabet *O* and, within it, the silhouette of a smiling bikini-clad lady, photographed from the front, lying sideways, with her head supported by her hand and long black hair obscuring her elbow. Last-minute essentials were being loaded into the aircraft. Only that these weren't the usual airline-passenger materials. These were caskets of chocolate cakes, whiskey, rum, champagne, towels, swimwear, party gear, and all the necessities for a party of the rich and the famous. This was a specially designed A380 party plane, with special shock absorbers to permit a discotheque hall in the lower deck.

They were boarding Orson's private A380 jet, bound for India. Orson, the billionaire younger brother of Hedwig, had a smaller share in the profits if the Amateurs XI were to win.

"I can't help thinking I'm next in line for assassination after my younger brother Graeme! Might as well live fast and die while I'm young," said an obese, bald middle-aged

Englishman, with a face as big as a piece of ham. "I can't wait to return to India. Such a lovely, lovely country. Wait for the October heat season—that makes the country even lovelier!" He broke out in perfect Hindi, "Oh meri India, meri India."

Orson Dawson was hosting the postmatch celebrations aboard his private A380. Only that this wasn't full of passenger seats. Most of them had been removed. Instead, the top tier was fitted with a large Jacuzzi and swimming pool while the bottom tier's front half had been modified into a nightclub.

Instead of formally dressed airhostesses, he employed Playboy Bunnies, dressed in skimpy two-piece bikinis, to serve his drinks. "Wait till you hear them try and instruct you to fasten your seatbelts. They just resemble cute pussycats," he joked in an arrogant, careless manner.

This typified the man—Orson Dawson was a millionaire playboy. His guests tonight included all the cricketers of both the teams that played and a rock band for entertainment. Among the guests was the unmistakable figure of the match fixer, Adam.

The flight was to reach Bangalore City in sixty hours and then, after attending Preity Lahoria's engagement party the next day, was to return to the UK the morning after for the last and final match of this series.

All the cricket players of both teams attended, except Amay Indulkar. "This cricket is too glamorous, man! We are not so lucky in baseball. The best we can get are cheerleaders for after-dinner activities. You guys rock. I must import this sport to the United States," said Ice Cool.

"That's the whole idea," replied Landon. "Only just don't try to double-cross us and start a cricket Boston Tea Party on us one day." They laughed.

After takeoff, Orson removed his expensive suit and changed into beachwear trunks with the cartoon of a pirate on the back and an anchor on the front. He wore a ship captain's cap and, bare-chested, ordered, "Girls, my honey bunnies, come and get these hungry cricketers. Lavish them with food, drink, and love. Let the party begin."

At this command, thirty young shapely bikini-clad women emerged with trays containing drinks and provided them to the guests. Loud music began to play from the aircraft speakers.

After an hour of drinks and junk food, aided by the loud beats of the rock music, the cricketers were dancing with one another and the women at the discotheque room in a nightclub-like atmosphere on the bottom tier of the A380. Landon and Davidson were in the upper tier in the Jacuzzi, warming up over the skies. They saw a gorgeous Amelia in a tigress-skin-print swimsuit walk into the Jacuzzi. It perfectly hugged her well-shaped hips and her luscious curves and showed off her long well-toned legs.

"Smile, boys," she flirted.

Landon replied, "There's no guessing what fruit and vegetables you want to eat tonight, you hungry tigress. No man is safe tonight with you around in this mood." Their laughs were in unison, and Davidson again noticed the ongoing chemistry between them.

At this point, they were joined by Orson himself. A huge red towel around his back and in slippers, he was flanked by two of his playmates on either side. He slapped each one in turn on their buttocks, making a wet noise, and playfully told them, "Girls, scat. Uncle Orson has business to do with these policemen." They left him alone.

Orson got into the Jacuzzi. "Listen, I'm no fool. I know what you lot are up to. I am after that magic cricket bat just as much as you are. I know that something in the Nandi Hills forest contains the big clue. It is very rare for me to go hiking in the woods. I'm looking forwards to it. I call it Operation Manjula."

"What's Operation Manjula?" asked Davidson

"Well, my ancestor Hughie Dawson had a young friend called Vijay. His wife was called Manjula. The legend goes that Vijay later on took over the Shepherd's Triad duties during my ancestor's time. Vijay, very fluent in English and Latin, gave out a clue about where the bat lies somewhere in the forest. Manjula was entrusted with the duties of hiding the bat in a secure location. The legend goes that Manjula hid it with Vijay's ashes, at the time of his death in the nineteenth century," said Orson Dawson

"Now my big brother, Hedwig, has sent his two dumbass private detectives to find it. I have no hopes for them. I will go after this bat myself. And you are—ha ha ha—going to lead me to it," said Orson.

Orson continued, "We all know that I came up with the words *Operation Manjula* to make it sound attractive to the mission. Simply put—bottom line—Mr. Byragi has agreed to meet only you, Landon. I don't understand why you specifically—he could have chosen any one of us—but he chose you. There is a massive seven-star hotel on the hill that the engagement is slated to take place. We are all staying in that hotel. It should come, therefore, as no surprise to you that all eyes will be on your door, Landon. We all want that magic bat, and I am going to get it one way or another. Make no mistake about that. We will be following you once you leave your room for the forest, led by Mr. Byragi. Cricket has never been so interesting! I already have arranged for guides and elephants and global positioning satellite for my little treasure hunt."

With that, he gave a long, loud, arrogant laugh, ambled out of the Jacuzzi, and walked toward the bottom tier to join the nightclub.

The next night, the A380 touched down in the Bangalore City airport. The bus ride to the hotel, where the engagement was to take place that evening, was swift, avoiding the congested Bangalore traffic. It was Orson's own luxury hotel, which could accommodate over three thousand guests, upon Nandi Hills.

Chapter 17

Romance atop a Cool Hill Station

Landon stood alone at the main terrace beside the moss-coated granite walls, with full view of the surrounding cotton-wisp-like clouds noiselessly floating around him and the abutting surrounding hillocks with coffee plantation and green grass that resembled islands in the clouds. The serenity of the rising sun between the mountains in the distance, the pure air, helped ease all the tensions and stress that the previous busy weeks had imposed upon him. The only sounds heard were the occasional chirping of birds in these heaven-on-earth-like tranquil surroundings. He felt one with nature.

Now relaxed, he was confident that he was going to meet Byragi, the second member of the Shepherd's Triad, and locate a clue as to where in the world the magic cricket bat lay hidden, by tonight.

He thought he heard the distinct click of high-heeled shoes behind him. He felt the soft femininity of a gentle woman's hands massaging his deltoids from behind. He knew who it was and took a deep breath in and exhaled all the tensions of the past few days. It was Amelia. Her blue eyes and tall figure complemented the large blue frock she wore to sweat it out in the Indian summer sun. Her plunging neckline only added finesse to her well-toned body. What hand hath taken out a rib from Landon's body and created this beautiful creature?

Landon felt this was the right moment. He held her hands and softly whispered to her ear that he was going to sing for her. She smiled and felt goose bumps all over her body. Landon gazed into her soul and sang her Elton John's "Your Song." In their isolation, surrounded by the forest and the wildlife below, they felt like two intelligent species above the animal life below them, in a courtship ritual.

Landon held her hand, and they walked back to their hotel room. "Why are you so kind to me, pretty lady?" asked Landon. This unexpected adventure their lives had taken made Landon grateful that he had decided to rejoin the police force. If nothing—if he indeed failed to find the culprits in England or wherever they may be—at least he had found love again. And that was well worth coming back to the force.

Landon and Amelia looked into each other's eyes. They never spoke a word—it was all communicated by body language. Landon massaged the tips of Amelia's hair. Amelia pushed her head back, as if enjoying it. Landon moved forward for a kiss, and they kissed passionately. Amelia felt his palm slide upward on her thigh. Amelia felt as if it was the first summer rains upon a land brought to drought from the lack of romance, a tragic affliction for generation X. Landon was like a leg spinner, reviving the lost art of romance into the twenty-first century.

They made their way into their hotel room.

Landon kissed Amelia's hands, from her fingers all the way up her forearms, all the way up her arms and shoulders, all the way up her neck, and repeated it on the other side. Amelia groaned in pleasure at being slowly, but surely, devoured by the man she loved and respected and allowed it to proceed.

Landon removed his shirt and was soon barechested. He unhooked Amelia's frock and bra from her shoulders and began to nibble on her shoulders with his lips. Amelia's eyes were closed, her body turned on by the bullets of pleasure she was receiving. She was fully undressed and in Landon's arms, lying on her back, and Landon was kissing her breasts, her torso, her thighs—Amelia had never experienced so much romance in her life. The love was overwhelming; she began to shed a tear.

Landon asked her, "What's wrong, baby?"

She replied, "Most men only want one-night stands, and they just want quick, cheap sex for themselves. You are so respectful and loving to my being. I am just so tearful with happiness that I found you." They kissed passionately and smiled as they met each other's eyes and rolled around the large queen-size bed. She was particularly amazed that he had such mental strength to take romance to such heights.

Amelia loved the way Landon was so consensual, slow, reflecting Amelia's pace and feelings, kissing her out of love and not lust, giving her time to adapt to new situations, using light-hearted humor when taking short breaks between kissing the feminine curves of her torso, her shapely legs and her bust, being a confident leader—she felt like the luckiest woman on earth, being led by a masterful lover in Landon Beau. Indeed, only a gentleman like Landon could bring out the lady out of a woman in Amelia.

Landon asked for her consent if he could go further. She agreed. Landon asked her to lie down on the bed and was soon massaging her deep spot [*reference: The G spot and other discoveries about human sexuality by Ladas, Whipple and Perry, ISBN 0440130409*]. Within minutes, she began to groan in orgasmic pleasure, her sounds only drowned by the gentle noise of the monsoon rains outdoors. Landon continued it for an hour. Right at the end, Landon asked her permission if he could come. She allowed him to, and they came together in orgasm. The world outside appeared to freeze in time to allow the unison of two similar minds and bodies to celebrate their very existence on the planet. The world was a better place for the two of them.

Landon gave Amelia multiple orgasms all afternoon, and they celebrated their newfound love in the highest way possible.

Chapter 18

Operation Manjula

The engagement ceremony and party of Preity Lahoria and Akshay Singh was a huge affair. The actual ritual had taken place earlier in the afternoon. The Nandi seven-star luxury hotels had its first major party. It was attended by most of the old and present directors, producers, actors, and actresses of Bollywood. Ministers and politicians abounded. The fact that cricketers were involved brought in even more guests from the cricket world. Former and present international cricketers, of all nationalities from the main ten Test-playing nations, altogether numbering over ten thousand guests in the magnificent Nandi Hotel, added to the glitterati. Most of the top brass of India's two largest industries—Bollywood and cricket, a combined might of billions of immeasurable dollars—were all in one place.

The selection of food was awesome—from *mughlai biryani* to lamb *rogan josh* from the north, from chicken *kolhapuri* to lamb madras from the south, the entire length and breadth of Indian cuisine was on display. The desserts of *ras malais, jalebis*, and *semiya payasam* were the perfect finish. There were imported wines too.

The Indian media branded this event the biggest and most significant matrimonial union ever in Indian history—as it involved the union of Bollywood and cricket, two of India's biggest money-spinners, in debatable order as to which is more superior.

But the most noticeable aspect about the couple that Landon noticed was how sad Preity Lahoria was. This was supposed to be a day of joy for her. On the other hand, Akshay stood by the balcony with a cigarette in one hand, dressed in a brown suit, and a handful of *ladoos* in the other, boasting to his friends about his money he'd earned and the wickets he took in the two recent matches in London.

Some of the Bollywood stars, owners of the major 20/20 cricket leagues in India, were taking autographs from the cricketers. Other film stars were discussing lucrative 20/20 contracts with the annual Indian 20/20 league with the cricketers, worth millions of dollars.

Landon, as watchful as a hawk, was aware of these several subplots within this ceremony. New Bollywood movies would be made and broken with this union. Merchandise and magazines would sell on this union like hotcakes—not only in India but even in neighboring countries. Indian cricket would get its glamorous couple. In a country where sportsmen are treated like gods and film stars likewise, this truly was a prelude to a wedding made in heaven.

He noticed that Adam the match fixer, last seen in Manchester, was in a corner, talking to some shady men dressed in suits and dark glasses.

Landon noticed Cindy Fartington dancing with millionaires. She saw Landon and approached him and put her hand on his shoulder and said, "Landon, it's going to be mad. I'm throwing a wild party in London for the night before the Lord's game, in two days' time. Hedwig—bless his cotton socks—will be there. Sort of a prematch celebratory party. Both the teams are invited. Be a dear and bring your darling girlfriend along for it, will you?"

It was nearing midnight. Amelia was partying, enjoying the wine and the company of the glamour. This was right up her alley—the fashion displayed made her wish she had more space in her digital camera to store more images.

Landon had unfinished business—he had to await contact from Byragi, whoever he was. And he knew that he was being watched by Orson and Adam's men as to when Byragi would emerge to arrange a rendezvous with him.

Landon completed eating a plate of *rasmalai* dessert and made his way to place the plate on a table. He was met by a bearded Indian waiter, dressed in a white suit and wearing a Sikh's turban, who took his plate on his tray. "Autograph please, Landon *sahib*," said the waiter and handed Landon a sheet of paper. Except that this was not an empty sheet of paper. These were instructions.

Scrolled across were instructions: "This is Byragi. Please do not get alarmed. Follow me out of the hall, through the restrooms." It was followed by a figure of a Shepherd's cane as a signature.

Landon noticed that both Amelia and Bob Davidson were not around. He followed the waiter to the men's room. The waiter threw his tray into the bin. He opened one of the latrine doors and turned a coat hook that masqueraded as a lever—a larger door appeared to be hinged from behind the latrine that opened, leading to the main balcony.

They ran outside, closing the secret entrance behind them. There was no security about. It seemed like a steep drop from the balcony downward. Landon saw Amelia and Bob down there already.

"How did . . ." said Landon, only to get interrupted by Byragi.

"Silence. Orson has a whole army of henchmen in the forest, on horses, elephants, and with global positioning satellite, waiting for me to lead you to the Enchanted Willow." Byragi pulled out his false beard and false turban disguise to reveal an exotic young Afro Indian woman, aged in her twenties, about five feet six inches tall, and with long curly black hair falling up to her waist. She untied a rope across her torso, and it stood perfectly erect vertically, without support—like magic, as if it had a life of its own—leading from the balcony to the ground.

"Indian rope trick," she said and asked Landon to climb down, and he did so. Landon could feel the cold night air, the sounds of night owls and crickets chirping in the dark, and the forest in front of them, freshly watered from the Indian monsoon rains of that afternoon. Byragi followed him. After they had climbed down, the rope just collapsed to the ground.

"Allow me to introduce myself, Landon, but we will soon get followed by their gang. Byragi is a bit too old for this sort of thing. My name is Masaba. I am the daughter of a great cricketer from the West Indies. You may remember that one member of the Shepherd's Triad also exists in the Caribbean. Well, it's about time they had women!"

Masaba, Bob Davidson, Amelia Kanowski, and Landon Beau fled into the Indian forest in the darkness.

Chapter 19

Adventure in the Indian Forest

The four entered the Indian forest at midnight. Masaba was wearing a baseball cap with an LED light to guide her across the forest. She broke a low-lying tree branch and used it to clear the dense vegetation. Amelia saw bats through the full moon above her. They heard a distant feline growl. "Must be an angry tiger," said Masaba, matter-of-factly. Landon felt Amelia holding on to him; he held on to her hand.

Davidson felt his dinner jacket, formal pants, and black shoes soaked through. They passed by sleeping birds, croaking frogs and their eggs, wild orchids, bugs and insects of every kind, shallow streams, a few snakes, and then a long-tailed chameleon. Landon played and hissed at the upset chameleon before placing him back on the branch. After about half an hour, deep into the forest, they heard the loud, trumpeting sound of an elephant.

"We may have stumbled across a herd," said Masaba. She was mistaken. A plethora of large artificial lights suddenly switched on, and they were surrounded by over two hundred people. They were largely on foot, on horseback, or with guide dogs. They saw the elephant in front of them. The rider of the elephant was none other than—Orson. And standing beside the elephant, dressed in a tracksuit, was Adam.

Orson overconfidently addressed Landon. "Well, well, well, Landon, my boy. You forgot to say 'Good-night and sleep tight' to me after the party!" And with it, he burst into a loud roll of self-applauding laughter and announced, "We will be following you to the ends of the earth. I want that magic bat. You will find it for me."

Orson was dressed in a jungle safari suit, with a rifle strung across his torso, and wearing a felt cowboy hat. He had a bottle of wine in one hand and one of his airhostesses in another. "Let the games begin!" he screamed and shot several bullets into the nighttime forest skies.

Adam the match fixer quipped, "Hey, Landon, we can't be kept out of the game, can we? We are dying to know whether you will find that magic bat. We can make fresh calculations in the bookie and betting world if you do. Like—Landon one hundred runs not out when he bats with it? Good luck."

The disruption of circadian rhythms with Orson's rifle shots and massive searchlights disturbed the habitat of the jungle. The confusion of the lights made the birds think it was day, and they began to take to take flight, and the bats began to hide for cover.

Masaba addressed Orson and his group, "Sorry to disappoint you, gentlemen, but the bat is not in India."

Those words made Orson freeze. The cigar dropped from his mouth onto his trousers. "What? I organized this extensive expedition to retrieve the bat. And you tell me that the bat is not here."

He fired two more shots in the air in frustration.

"We will still follow you to see what you will find," replied Orson.

The jungle trek went on for two hours into the night.

Masaba spoke to Landon, "The legend goes that the match fixers were jailed in India after being found guilty of first-degree murder in 1810. They were released, and they wasted away into alcoholism, solitude, and worthlessness, eventually dying of no honor.

"Vijay left a message, engraved on a rock. He wanted his ashes to be kept there when he died. His dutiful wife, Manjula, delivered his ashes to that rock that we are heading to now. It is the key to understanding where the bat lies."

"What of the message?" asked Landon.

"Well, it was written in Latin. It is hidden and was only to be revealed in cricket's greatest hour of need. It gives a vital hint of where the magic bat lics."

They reached a collection of large boulders at the edge of the forest. They were followed by the two hundred men and Orson mounted atop an elephant. The full consortium and Orson's army did not notice another unidentified group of two individuals following their larger group behind them.

"Not far now," said Masaba. She pointed to a large banyan tree, with roots that reached from the branches to the ground. They reached to the tree and stood next to the two boulders placed side by side of each other. She pulled what appeared to be one of the branches taking root into the soil. The boulders gave way and opened into a hearth underground. It looked like the entrance to a secret cave.

"Here it is. Let's enter," ordered Masaba.

Orson was scared to enter the dark cave. "Err . . . you go, Landon. You have to come out at some point, eventually. We'll be waiting here, to take from you what you bring out for us. Ha ha ha!"

Landon, Masaba, Amelia, and Bob entered the cave. The boulders shut behind them.

Landon smelled the damp air of the soil moistened by the monsoon rains. Byragi had a flashlight, and they noticed stone-engraved stairs leading to the inner recesses of this cave. Its walls were full of cobwebs and dead insects.

"This is the burial site of the ashes of Vijay of the Shepherd's Triad," said Masaba.

In the light, they approached a piece of shining sandstone. A marble jar held what appeared to be the ashes of Vijay. On the jar were inscribed these words:

Cura reperitur in morbum

Landon and Bob took pictures of this with their iPhones. Amelia, who studied basic Latin in school, was able to decipher the words to mean "The cure will be found within the disease" in English. These words were written by Vijay, well versed in English and Latin, the friend of Hughie Dawson, over one hundred years ago, at the time of his death.

As soon as they finished clicking the pictures, they heard a scream. Masaba was kicked from behind, and she fell forward, knocking the light onto the ground. Her cap fell off her head, and the LED light shining forward cast a light upon the direction of the attacker and an even more massive shadow backward of the attacker, who was already eight feet tall. It looked like a scene from Beowulf.

Amelia screamed. Landon recognized the attacker.

It was Slocum, the New Zealand assassin.

Her scream wasn't loud enough for the crowd waiting outside to hear. Slocum took a step toward Davidson and grabbed him by the throat, using his left hand. He turned on his electronic voice device, which gave the chilling message while Bob was fighting the grasp on his throat. "Now I want to hear you screammmm!"

Landon desperately tried to free Davidson, but Slocum's huge right arm brushed him aside. And he fell onto the walls of the cave, landing on his back.

Slocum looked at Amelia and pressed his electronic voice device to issue her with a chilling warning. "You're next, poppet."

Masaba had an old-fashioned wooden catapult in her pocket. She took a nearby stone, aimed for Slocum's left eye, and secured a direct hit with the stone. Slocum let go of Inspector Davidson, dropped him to the ground, and began to howl in agony. Amelia gathered Inspector Davidson, and they fled with Landon and Masaba, leaving behind a yelping Slocum.

"How do we get out?" asked Amelia.

"There is another exit that leads to the other side of the forest. Probably that's how he entered in," said Masaba.

They crawled through a tunnel, and after an hour of tiresome crawling, they reached the opening at the outer edge of the forest. Masaba had already arranged a getaway vehicle.

A Mitsubishi minivan was waiting for them.

"Get in, and go to the airport quickly. A Singapore Airlines flight has been booked to take the three of you back to London. Your luggage has already been checked in. It leaves in an hour," said Masaba. "It was nice meeting you all."

"What about Orson?" asked Landon.

"He'll literally see the light of day soon enough. In any case, she's waiting for you in England. She will help you find the magic bat."

"Who's she?" asked Landon. The van was about to depart in full speed for the international airport. They barely had time to listen to Masaba's last few words, "She has already met you. She's our boss," as the van sped off to the airport in the majestic Indian dawn.

Chapter 20

*Finding the Enchanted Willow
in the Haunted House*

The 747 touched down at Heathrow. Throughout the flight, Landon could not sleep well—he kept thinking of who this person was who was going to be the great hope in London. The person described by both the members of the Shepherd's Triad—first Jim and now Masaba. He could see blue eyes in his dream but was interrupted by the flight attendant's call to disembark.

Davidson, Amelia, and Landon were greeted by a smiling Inspector Harrison at the airport. "Well done, folks. Good news—another breakthrough from our end in toxicology. We have identified the poison in the coach's system. It seems that he was ingesting huge amounts of selenium."

"Selenium?" said Bob.

"Yes, a naturally occurring element that can only be either deliberately ingested or inadvertently fed. He did complain of feeling ill to his teammates just before the match. But he's still in suspended animation."

"What could have caused that?" asked Bob.

"We still have that mystery to solve," answered Inspector Harrison. "But with proper hemodialysis that he is receiving presently, he should be able to lose the toxin out of his system and get better."

"What's in other news?" asked Landon.

"Well, the Chinese officials are very keen on importing cricket to China. They wish the final match at Lord's would get televised broadcast to their one billion viewers in their country on state-controlled television! Huge success and popularity for our humble game! They are apparently very impressed with Ling Zhang-Hue's wicket-keeping. Not bad for a soccer goalkeeper.

"As for gossip, the arranged marriage between Preity Lahoria and Akshay Singh is scheduled for this Saturday, soon after the Lord's match, in two days' time. The ceremony and banquet are to be held at the Castle Guard Hotel, overlooking the Thames River in Reading."

"What about the magic bat?" asked Harrison.

"This is the weird part. Someone is supposed to meet me here in London. It's supposed to be a woman, I'm told by the Shepherd's Triad. Don't know who it is yet or when they'll initiate contact. I'll just play the waiting game," replied Landon.

"The rest of your team and the Professionals XI will be arriving tonight from the Bangalore party. Hedwig was desperately trying to reach you. He didn't say why."

"Nothing bad, perhaps," said Landon.

They were greeted by the robotic figure of Skittle at the baggage carousel. "Your baggage will arrive in approximately five minutes and thirty-seven seconds, Mr. Landon," it announced.

What the hell is Skittle doing here? thought Landon. As if to answer, the figure of an angry Hedwig Dawson approached.

"I approached all the proper channels, and you cannot fault me for not doing so," he fumed. "You run off in my brother's luxury airliner to India without informing me. How dare you! What did that creep have to tell you?"

"Mr. Dawson, with all due respect, we did meet your executive secretary at the party there. She might be able to tell you more. It was a team-bonding event. We were also admittedly after the magic bat. We were following a lead. Well, we failed to retrieve it," replied Landon.

"Did you say you *failed*?" said Hedwig Dawson. "I do not employ people who fail. This is not how to get onto my good side."

With that, he turned and abruptly left, followed by his android secretary, Skittle. Skittle's last few words, forever meaningless, could be heard, "Have a nice day."

An exhausted, fatigued, and sleep-deprived Landon was tucked into bed by a caring Amelia. Later that evening, he awoke, and they went for a jog around Abbotts's Orchard. Landon and Amelia shared gentle stories of their lives. They were starting to bond on an emotional and romantic level.

Landon's iPhone rang to its characteristic tune of Bon Jovi's hit song from 2000, "It's My Life." It was an unknown number. The caller identified herself as Lucy. He remembered her as the jogger at the Oval who promised to contact him after he had returned from India.

"How did you get my number?" asked an exasperated Landon.

"It was given to me by your shop assistant in Hindley Green," she replied cheerfully. She continued, "How would you like to go on an adventure and recover the Enchanted Willow tonight?"

Landon was speechless. Amelia noticed the shock in his eyes.

Lucy continued, "Landon, you are getting very close to solving the case. Your positive thinking, intelligence, and faith in God have rewarded you with these opportunities. Just go with them. Go with the flow."

"Where can we meet?" asked Landon.

"Sip of coffee at Knightsbridge at the Persona Pub this evening at around half eight. Then we leave for the house where the Willow is kept."

"Where is this house? Can we not go there at once?" asked Landon.

Lucy hung up. Landon informed the inspectors of this possible new lead.

That night, at eight p.m., Inspector Davidson, Landon and Amelia met with their new ally at Knightsbridge. She was dressed in a black sweater, black jeans, trainers, and had her hair tied in a ponytail.

"Who are you again?" asked Inspector Davidson. "Lucy, of the Department of Medieval History, University of Leeds. I track down lost artifacts. I've been tracing the Enchanted Willow through history."

"Oh really?" said Landon. "How far does it go back?"

Lucy explained, "St. Sebastian of the Roman era. He was the patron saint of many things, but two among them are ironmongers and sport."

Lucy continued, "The Enchanted Willow contains a piece of cylindrical metal called Penta that was made and blessed by St. Sebastian himself. It was thought to be lost, only to be rediscovered in a church around the eighteenth century by a young soldier called Dawson. He was fighting in the Crimean War and soon found out that he never got hit by bullets in the war if he carried it with him. In order to prevent it from falling into the wrong hands, he hid Penta inside a wooden cricket bat. Being the patron saint of sports, that bat was conferred with magical properties because of Penta—the person batting with it never got out."

The gasps of wonder from Landon and Davidson could be heard by Amelia at that profound remark from Lucy. Landon felt adrenaline surging through his body, at the prospect of soon being able to find the Enchanted Willow.

Lucy continued, "The bat is magical, remember? It was used by Baron Dawson, his son, to score that huge county cricket first-class score of 501 not out in 1833 despite him coming close to retirement and aged nearly fifty."

"So where is it now?" asked Landon.

"My research indicates that it is in England, in the outskirts of London, in a derelict building. We can leave for it straightaway."

She sat in the front seat of Davidson's police car and seemed bubbly and excitable. She seemed to know all the directions and confidently led the trio to an abandoned castle on the outskirts of London. They were soon within the countryside, driving across narrow roads, without a map or global positioning satellite to guide them. They did not notice that they were being followed.

"This is Hempstead Villa," she explained, and they drove through the front gates and wild uncut grass that surrounded this abandoned castle. "The bat lies here, according to my research," said Lucy.

Landon was bewildered. "How on earth? Why did we have to travel all the way to India, according to the Shepherd's Triad, if you say the bat is here? In this derelict old ruin of a house?"

Lucy replied, "What did that inscription on the marble say?"

Landon wondered at how this stranger knew so much. "Now that's classified information. It was written in Latin, but translated into English, it meant that 'the cure will be found within the disease.'"

"Exactly!" said Lucy. "The disease is match fixing in cricket. We also now have a murder mystery to solve. And the cure—is the magic bat. Like it did countless times before, it will do it again. This happens to be the former home of the slain match fixer, Brian Cashman, over two hundred years ago. He was pure evil in his every fabric. He lived here. Dawson's ancestor wanted to hide the magic bat to the best of his ability. That is the meaning of the message you read in India—the bat is to be found in this house."

Amelia added, "This house is *also* believed to be haunted."

They approached the house. Amelia clasped Landon's hand tightly. "Landon, how I wish we got lost on the roads. I'm soooo not looking forward to this. I have a bad feeling about this. Landon, please tell me that it's going to be all right."

Landon held her hand reassuringly, and they were led by Lucy into the front door of Hempstead House. The front door was missing, and there was no electricity supplying the house.

They smelled the damp, moss-soaked walls and decaying wood. They heard thunder outside. "Oh, just some welcome June drizzle," said Lucy. Davidson drew his semiautomatic. The detectives entered the house after them.

"What do we use for a light?" said Landon.

"A torch!" said Lucy, who came well prepared. Lucy lit her torch. She confidently led them upstairs into the piano room.

Landon, Amelia, and Davidson were all in awe of Lucy's sheer confidence in finding her way in a derelict house. "They have good maps in the library," she explained. The staircases squeaked at each step they took. She entered the piano room on the third floor. An old piano stood there with a solitary chair in the darkness. The thick dust and abundance of cobweb covering had indicated that it hadn't been used in years to play music.

Amelia wished in her mind, *Please don't play, please don't play.*

As if for reply, a peal of thunder was heard outside to frighten Amelia as she hung onto Landon more closely. Landon patted her on the back reassuringly. "It's all right, darling. Feel safe with me."

Another flash of lightening lighted the room for almost ten seconds. Lucy pointed to a human-sized picture frame on the wall and shouted, "There, that's him! The world is a better place without him." It had the life-size portrait of an evil-looking man, bald, with long gray hair on the back of his head. Below were the words Brian Cashman.

Landon walked toward the poster. Lucy took out a Swiss army knife and slashed the picture obliquely, from one top corner to the other bottom corner. Another flash of lightning filled the room—and Landon, Bob, and Amelia gasped at what lay behind the portrait.

Serenely nestled behind the portrait was the object they came to find. It was the Enchanted Willow—they had found the magic bat.

Chapter 21

The Enchanted Willow

They were consumed by a feeling of divine mercy. A sacred artifact from the Roman times, blessed by Saint Sebastian, adapted to cricket, and preserved in its humble angelic glory into the twenty-first century. The bottom third of the bat that appeared missing was the piece that was on display in the Orson Dawson museum. The rest of the bat looked a bit yellowish from age, and Landon found it to be quite small and lightweight.

They turned to leave. They heard the abrupt closure of the door they were standing in front of. A humongous, eight-foot-tall figure was blocking their exit. It was the New Zealand assassin, Slocum, again.

This time, he had an eye patch, secondary to the injury earned in India. He turned on his electronic device to speak on his behalf again. This time, it said, "Ladies first," and proceeded to walk toward Amelia.

Landon blocked his path. "You go through me first!" he said.

He grasped Landon's throat in an instant. He turned on his device, which said, "You like to sing, do you? You sing on Youtube.com so well. Now I want to hear you sing for me."

Slocum continued, "Now sing 'Aaah' for me and die!" and squeezed Landon's throat harder.

Amelia took cover as Bob fired two shots into Slocum's shoulders, with minimal effect.

"Let him go, Slocum, the next one's into your brains. We will fire out of self-defense."

Amelia was engulfed in a frenzy of chagrin at the fearful monster choking her man yet felt so helpless.

At this point, Lucy stood forward. "This charade has gone on for too long." She lifted her hands and pointed a finger toward Slocum. Slocum froze, his muscles wobbled, and he dropped a still-alive Landon onto the floor. Amelia grabbed Landon on the floor.

"Amelia and Bob, will you please drag him away immediately?" Her steely blue eyes were giving purposeful directions and a direct stare into Slocum. Slocum had a surprised look on his face. He couldn't move. Bob and Amelia got Landon closer to Lucy's direction. Suddenly, they felt a blaze of fire. The floor beneath Slocum opened and revealed flames of Hell. Slocum had no time to scream as he dropped hellward, and the floor sealed up. The last of Slocum was his electronic voice screaming, "Helppp . . . !"

Slocum was no more.

The only problem now was that the house was on fire.

They rushed downstairs, Amelia and Davidson carrying Landon between them, and fled out of the house, taking the magic bat along with them. They reached outdoors, where the rain had stopped. The house was now engulfed in flames.

"What was that? Where's Slocum?" asked Amelia.

"Oh, he just dropped below" was Lucy's simple reply. They were at a loss to explain what they had just seen. They were only satisfied that Slocum was no longer in the equation of this crime.

Lucy said to them, "Bob, Landon, and Amelia—drive back to HQ."

Bob replied, "But what about you? We can't possibly leave a lady alone in the countryside this time in the night. Come with us."

Lucy was steadfast in her decision. "No, I'll stay here. I need to call the fire engines. I have my mobile. I can call for help. You now have a historical artifact in your possession. Use it to help your out-of-form batsmen to regain form in the next two days. If the police find you now, they'll think you burnt down the house deliberately to recover this bat. Now go."

"But *we are* the police," Bob reminded her.

Lucy replied, "Bob, for heaven's sake, go. I'll meet you in two days' time for a farewell when you play the third and final match at Lord's. See you then."

Bob concluded, "One last thing. Dial 999 and ask for Agent 3127, if you require any assistance." And he drove off toward London, with Landon recovering in the backseat in Amelia's arms. They met a fire brigade, travelling in the opposite direction to theirs, making its way toward the burning house.

Amelia and Bob wondered what just happened. It had all happened so fast. They could scarcely comprehend the pace of the recent events. Landon groaned in agony as he lay over Amelia's lap in the backseat, still breathing.

As they drove off into the darkness, they passed a hill. The clouds had cleared, and they saw—through the background of the full moon rising behind that hill, a couple of kilometers away into the moors—a thin, tall man standing, dressed in a cloak, holding a shepherd's cane, watching their car speed away.

Chapter 22

Net Practice at Lord's

Back at HQ, the next day, Inspector Harrison's face had jubilation written all over it.

"We are starting to solve the case now. Things are going in our favor. Firstly, Graeme Dawson no longer has any selenium in his body now. Our antidotes have fixed this. Our doctors are working on how to reverse this suspended animation that he's in. He should soon be conscious and able to speak to us about what really happened at the hotel room that night.

"Secondly, the death of Slocum is a huge plus. He really was a moron and a murderer who hailed from Gore in New Zealand. Does that make him a 'Goron'? I don't know.

"Thirdly, this magic bat you have so ably retrieved will help our Amateurs XI batsmen gain batting form. This should help us win the final match and give us the series win 2-1. This will help restore all the profits for the Dawson Corporation. Hedwig Dawson will be pleased, and he finally gets off my back."

Inspector Davidson said, "All we need to know now is who tried to murder Graeme Dawson. Slocum died without telling us who he was working for."

Sir Nigel concluded, "The final match is in two days' time. Practice well."

The Amateurs XI team meeting took place at the visitor's dressing room at Lord's Cricket Ground in London. Landon, the captain of the Amateurs XI, addressed his team, "Teammates. Watch this video."

He played a video of Sir Don Bradman with the background songs of Paul Kelly. After seeing the five-minute clip, he told his team, "Sir Don, God bless his soul, was the greatest cricketer who ever lived. All the others are measured by his standards. Sir Don wasn't interested in breaking records. All he wanted to do was to bat to the best of his ability each time. An out-of-form batsman once approached Sir Don and asked how to get his batting form back, and Sir Don replied that he had to simply hit the ball along the ground. You see, you won't score any runs and win matches if you get out and are sitting in the pavilion. The bowlers are trying to get you out—you have to fight fire with fire and use your hand skills and intelligence out there in the middle. Just do your very best for just this one game, and don't worry about the result. The result will take care of itself.

"I have with me here a magic bat. It is called the Enchanted Willow. I want each and every one of you to bat with it and score lots and lots of runs doing so. The bowlers can take turns bowling to the batsmen and try and get them out. Just take the magic bat and see how it will allow you to score runs.

"Zhang-Hue and Indulkar get first priority, as Indulkar needs to get a hundred for us on top of the order as an opener and Zhang-Hue comes from a non-cricket-playing country. Third in line, I believe, is Ice Cool—to learn to play some actual cricket shots and perfect them. The baseball shots are good, but I'll teach you the cover drive, the on drive, the off drive, the hook shot, the pull shot, the cut, the French cut, and teach you to play shots on both sides of the wicket, off front and back foots.

"Our IT team has composed videos of you all from the previous match in your good points—Ling might want to watch his brilliant catch taken as wicket-keeper off the bowling of Chris Dawson. Inspector Davidson's good cover drive, Milton Keans's yorker to the Professionals XI—just enjoy the videos accompanied by the music. And let's go out there and enjoy our practice session and win a game of cricket!"

They left for the field and bonded over the course of the day.

After an hour of batting with the magic bat, Indulkar started to feel confident again of his batting. The bowling machine bowled at 100 miles per hour, and Indulkar was confidently connecting sixes and fours to short-pitched bowling, using the pull shot and the hook shot. Indulkar started to play pull strokes and back-foot strokes more confidently. The magic bat was used by Ice Cool, who started to play proper cricketing strokes and appreciated that he could play one of his baseball hoicks if need be. Ling Zhang-Hue got batting practice. He heard Landon cheer him loudly, "Zhang, my friend, you are keeping the wickets beautifully." The bowlers were bowling a consistent line and length. Confidence was building. The team was bonding.

After the day's practice, Indulkar was on his way to catch the train back home. He was met at the train station by Preity Lahoria. She had a yellowed sheet of paper that had Indulkar's autograph on, preserved for over fifteen years. She gave the piece of paper to him. She said, "Love your batting, Amay."

He replied, "I'll score a hundred for you day after tomorrow."

At the press conference, Amelia saw Landon and Bob answering the reporters with a straight bat on questions of match fixing, morale of the team, form of the team, their trips to India for parties despite losing, the batting form of Indulkar, the batting form of Landon, the potency of the bowling attack to restrict the Professionals XI for under two hundred runs in twenty overs, and so on. She was focused on Landon's body language, the way he tackled the questions from the reporters, his confidence—she felt empowered seeing all this.

Landon and Amelia had an intimate dinner that night. In the candle light, Amelia asked Landon how he was keeping up with so much of travel and solving a crime and captaining a cricket team. Landon said, "I feel in form. I could not have done it without you. You are my guardian angel. I love you."

They departed into the London evening in each other's arms.

Chapter 23

Final Day Before the Final Match

The newspapers predicted a full house at Lord's for the morrow. A large Chinese delegate and fan presence was expected to watch Ling Zhang-Hue in action.

The magic bat had successfully got all the Amateurs XI batsmen in good form.

The prematch dinner party was hosted at Orson Dawson's Wimbledon resort. The cricketers from both teams attended. At the party, they saw Adam and Cindy Fartington. Orson approached Landon. "Can't you say good-bye like a good boy? Why did you have to leave us in the jungle full of mosquitoes, standing by those boulders all night, in India in the summer?"

Orson Dawson continued, "Forget Hedwig and this prematch party of his. You are invited to my place as well, you know. I have a two-meter Red Sea shark and a two-meter Nile crocodile in my basement. We plan tonight to pit the two of them in battle. I think the crocodile is smarter than the shark and might bite off a fin and cause it to bleed to death. Won't you join me and my honey bunnies and friends for this clash of titans tonight?"

Landon excused himself and walked away.

Toward the end of the party, Cindy Fartington, partially drunk, waited all night for Amelia to take a toilet break and then approached Landon. She put her hands on Landon's neck, and he felt her sharp scratch upon the back of his neck as she drew him hungrily close to her face.

Cindy Fartington said, "You would look good playing the game without your colored clothes on. Why don't you just bowl and captain your team in underwear for me? If you take a wicket, I'll throw my 100,000-pound Victoria's Secret angel-wings bra and pink panties at your feet and lap dance for you. Come to my home, and sleep with me tonight, will you? I'm bored, I'm feeling horny, and I'm getting old. I could do with a shag from a nice young bullock like you."

Landon courteously excused her manners as one of harmless flirting and excused himself.

The guests were leaving. Landon wanted his team to have an early night. They had to focus on the big match tomorrow. Bob, Amelia, and Landon sat on an after-dinner settee near the poolside, thinking of having one last drink.

They ordered tea. Amelia ordered green herbal tea, her favorite. A waiter brought the tea.

Amay Indulkar was having a drink, chatting away with McNally. At the corner of his eye, he could make out the rotund figure of a man with a French beard and waddling gait approaching him. It was Adam.

The London full moon in the air-conditioned room made this bookmaker's voice and ambience chilling. "Boss, boss, you cricketer, boss? Boss, boss, money for you. You get out for zero runs, earn million rupees, okay, boss? You drop one catch, half a million more for you. You don't do as I tell you, you and your family die!" He left a shaken Indulkar behind.

Amay went to report this to Landon, who quickly ran outside to meet Adam. "You creep, that's enough. Why do you harass that boy? He hasn't done anything wrong!"

Adam replied, "Ha ha! Just joking. You have no proof."

Landon said, "I can arrest you for these—death threats."

Adam got out of the car and thrust his wrists out. "Go ahead. Like I told you in Manchester, they will only send in a dozen more." Adam got into his car and drove off into the darkness.

Akshay Singh approached the Amateurs XI batsmen. "I am feeling so powerful. I will bowl 100 miles per hour and bounce the buggery out of all of you. I can't wait to bowl at you tomorrow. Then more money, more wickets, and a wedding in Wimbledon first and Mumbai later! Life is such a party."

Chris Dawson approached Landon's group, Amelia and Davidson. "Hey guys, you haven't seen my dad's place yet. He has a collection of wildlife let loose into the park this time of the night. You could see them using my night-vision goggles." He snapped his fingers, and a waiter brought over three pairs of night-vision goggles to the group.

They put on the goggles. Through the darkness of the night, they saw antelopes, foxes, bears, gazelles, and buffalos roam the gardens. As the three watched in separate directions, Amelia's line of sight caught a human figure in the bushes. She wondered what this person was doing there. The human figure kneeling down on one knee had a large cylindrical object in his hands. She knew what this meant—a hunter.

She turned back to tell Landon and Bob Davidson. She only found Davidson sitting next to her. She looked out into the parklands—there was Landon, walking to get a closer look at the wildlife. She put two and two together. This was not a hunter. Someone was out to shoot Landon dead.

Amelia screamed, "Landon, run!"

Landon turned back to hear his beloved's voice. "What's wrong, honey?" He heard the gunshot.

The bullet scraped past his coat and got lodged into his iPhone in his left shirt pocket. Landon thought he was going to die, only that he was surprised to find himself alive on the ground despite taking a bullet near his heart.

Davidson took out his semiautomatic and urged Amelia to get down. Using the night-vision goggles, he could make out an attacker fleeing into the darkness. He shouted across, "Landon, are you okay?"

"Alive, not hurt," replied Landon. Davidson and Landon, with night-vision goggles on, gave chase into the night. They thought they could catch up with their attacker, but he was too quick for them. The attacker left behind the automatic rifle.

Amelia caught up with the pair, along with the hotel security. Landon wore a glove and picked up the rifle. He examined it closely, especially near the operator's end.

"What are you looking at?" asked Inspector Davidson.

Amelia saw Landon's face light up. He had that look on his face when he had his moments of brilliance.

Landon knowingly replied, "Call off the search for the getaway vehicle. Waste of our resources. I know the person who tried to kill Graeme Dawson. I have this case all sewn up. I will reveal it after we play and win the final match tomorrow."

Chapter 24

Lord's Cricket Ground — Final Match

The Amateurs XI wore blue-colored outfits, and the Professionals XI wore red. The MCC members wore their characteristic ties and jackets for this event. The spectators, knowing that his was a combination of all nationalities on either side, were rooting for the underdog, namely, the Amateurs. Their hopes were livened when they saw the name Amay Indulkar as confirmed to open the batting on the team list. There was music from the stands, with one rock song dedicated for each batsman. There were shapely cheerleaders dressed in the corresponding color outfits for each team. There were fireworks at the entrance of each gate where the players entered the field, which sent up a myriad of colored fires to greet each incoming batsman. The media box was full, with reporters preparing for the day ahead. Television cameras and sponsors' boardings surrounded the boundary ropes for this match. The predominant contingent in the crowd were Indian spectators, cheering for Amay Indulkar.

Overall, it was a carnival atmosphere of 20/20 to accompany the serious business of the cricket match.

The series was 1-1, and the sun bathed Lord's under a cloudless sky. Father Time, the iconic weather vane, was motionless, indicating perfect conditions for cricket, and the main clock struck 10:00 a.m. The full-house atmosphere greeted the toss. Landon Beau called correctly. He decided to field first, putting the Professionals XI team in to bat.

This was indeed very surprising. Traditional cricketing logic demanded that when in doubt, bat first. Landon decided to field first instead.

Just at the start of the match was yet another turn of events. The Amateurs XI dressing room was visited by two VIPs with the tag ICC on their suits. One introduced himself as Arun Lorgat, the other as Malcolm Fast.

"Can we speak to the captain please?" They met up with Landon Beau.

Malcolm Fast began, "Mr. Beau, we are from the International Cricket Council. As you know, we govern the game globally. Every single first-class match played anywhere in the world is under our supervision."

Mr. Lorgat continued, "I am its president, and Malcolm here is my deputy. We are under the impression that you have some sort of a magic bat in this room that you intend to use for the game."

Landon felt his heart sink.

Landon politely admitted, "I'm not one of those to break the rules. I'm a law enforcement officer myself. Do you gentlemen wish to take the bat away?"

Lorgat said, "Ah, yes, please. We believe that this is a much sought-after historical artifact and should be best placed in a museum. I'll keep the bat for now and give it back to you after the game."

After the ICC officials left, Davidson fumed, "Now how are we going to bat? We have lost our magic bat."

Landon's reply was astounding. "Bob, I wasn't intending to use it for batting today. Besides, we are fielding first. Let's concentrate on restricting their scoring, taking their wickets, holding on to our catches—basically doing the simple things right. We will worry about how we bat after the lunch interval."

Landon's last words to his team as they prepared to enter the field of play were "Team, I am soooo proud of you. You have performed so very well in practice. To the bowlers—line and length. Fielders, hold on to your catches and dive and save runs. It gives such a huge morale boost to the fielding side. Let's play to the best of our ability."

Chris Dawson had the new ball and opened the bowling with Keans.

Over number 2.0: The Professionals XI openers had raced to 20 runs. Dawson bowled an inswinger into the opener that took the outside edge and flew to first slip, where it was caught by the all-rounder McNally. Score became 20/1.

Over number 3.4: Dawson appealed for a leg-before-wicket decision against the Professionals XI number 3, a good inswinger. He's been given out by the umpire. The score was 22/2.

Overs number 3.5 and 3.6: Two crashing off-side drives for 4 runs takes the score to 30/2 after 4 overs.

Over number 5.3: The Professionals XI number 4 batsman is bowled by the out swinger from Dawson. They are tethering at 43/3.

Over number 6.2: Ray Shade lands the off-spinner into the blind spot of the opening batsman and was judged to be leg before wicket by umpire Harold Birds. Score 54/4.

Orson Dawson was in the stadium in a VIP box with two of his Playboy playmates. He teased them, "What's that called? Leg before wicked!" They gestured rudely toward an angry Hedwig Dawson. He was seated next to Skittle, who kept him informed of business transactions. Sitting to his left was none other than Cindy Fartington, in stony cold silence, watching the match without any emotions.

Orson joked with the playgirls. "His robot secretary Skittle has a computer console in her bust. Hedwig was always very poor with the ladies. I wonder what he does in his spare time with her. The first such case in the world of a human— robot . . ." And the playgirls giggled with Orson as they pointed to a perplexed Hedwig Dawson, who in turn glared back at them, wondering what they were laughing at.

Over number 7.3: Batsman nicks an edge off McNally's reverse swing to wicket-keeper Zhang-Hue. The Chinese contingents were jubilant at the diving catch to his right. Live images of that catch got beamed to China, bringing lots of happiness to China. Score: 65/5.

The Professionals XI staged some sort of a recovery by reaching 102/5 by the twelfth over.

Over number 12.2: Shade bowls. Batsman swept, did not connect. Got a top edge, caught by Rickards in the deep. Score: 102/6. Akshay Singh came out to bat.

Over number 14.3: He took the score up to 118/6. At that stage, Akshay tried to hit a straight ball out of the ground to midwicket, but it was caught by Indulkar, running with his back toward the ball, much to Akshay's disgust. Score 118/7.

Over number 15: McNally bowled a slower ball that induced the opposition team's wicket-keeper to hit one straight back to him and got a caught and bowled. 128/8.

Over number 18: Keans's yorker went right through the tailender and uprooted the leg-stump, 135/9.

Over number 19: Last man came out of his crease, down the wicket to hit Shade for 6, missed the ball, and Zhang gathered the ball behind the stumps and easily stumped him.

Score: Professionals XI all out for 143 in 19 overs.

Target for the Amateurs XI to win the match: 144 run off 20 overs.

Landon, satisfied with his team's bowling and fielding effort, his face beaming with pride, shouted, "Team, let's meet quickly after we have had something to eat and before we start batting!"

His intelligent field placing and marshalling of bowling resources had produced quite an astounding result. One hundred forty-four was a low total to chase, even in 20 overs of 20/20 cricket. Landon fancied his team's chances of winning the match and, with it, the series.

Milton Keans received physiotherapy to his back, the music was loud in the Amateurs XI room, and Amelia gave her lover Landon a quick kiss just before he took a shower.

After a quick lunch, the Amateurs XI met around their skipper, Landon. He said, "We have to think positively. They batted poorly in the morning, and we bowled a good line and length with enough variations to take their wickets. Whatever happens, I don't mind if you win or lose as long as you play to the best of your ability."

Indulkar approached Landon. "What about the match fixers?"

Landon replied, "This case took an interesting turn yesterday, when someone tried to shoot and kill me. I now know who the murderer of the coach is. I can assure you, the match fixers, at least for once, are innocent. And I know that the match fixers don't know of this yet—because I have kept the identity of the murderer to myself. When I reveal the murderer tomorrow morning, the world will know who did it, and I assure you that the match fixers will, in all likelihood, back off. So play your natural game. Imagine yourself scoring our victory runs. You are the best batsman we've got—all our hopes rest on you. You can do it. I'll open the batting with you, and we'll talk out there. Now get ready, Amay."

Akshay was in a foul mood and all fired up. How could he allow Amay, a poor boy from India, take a catch off his bat? He was determined to finish Amay Indulkar once and for all. He was the fastest bowler for the Professionals XI and could reach 91 miles per hour on a regular basis with his fast bowling. He ran in to bowl to Indulkar and peppered him with beamers and short deliveries.

He taunted Indulkar, "Hey, *baccha*, you don't score runs by ducking and weaving. Your bat must actually hit the ball to score. Why don't you get out and give me your wicket and get the next batsman in? Or else I'll make *masala dosa* out of you like I did in school."

He walked back to his bowling mark. Landon walked down the pitch and spoke to Amay. "Just imagine you have that magic bat in your hands. Play the hook and pull shot when he next bowls short. The faster the ball comes, the harder you hit it, as the Indian great Kapil Dev once said. You are such a good batsman. Do it for me." And he patted Indulkar on the back.

Preity Lahoria, who had attended the match with her father, was in tears, chewing at her shawl at the brutality shown to Amay by Akshay's intimidating fast bowling. She wore a blue T-shirt in support of her favorite batsman in the world, Amay Indulkar.

She closed her eyes and prayed heavenward, "Please, God, let Amay score runs."

Amay felt strong after hearing Landon's encouraging words. Akshay came running in again and bowled the ball in short. Amay played the hook shot with all his strength. The ball went soaring for six over square leg.

Akshay grunted and fumed. Preity was dancing in the aisles. Akshay motored in again, past the popping crease, and unleashed all his male energy and anger into one fast delivery that was short and up to Indulkar's head—Indulkar played at the ball using the pull shot at face level, and the ball went racing to the backward square leg boundary for four runs.

An angry Akshay didn't bother listening to his captain for changes in field positions. He motored in and bowled so short that the ball was above Indulkar's head—yet the little man managed to get the top edge of his bat to it, and the ball went flying over the wicket-keeper's head to the deep fine leg area for six more runs.

Akshay was pulling his hair out and squatted down the pitch. He accepted some field placement changes from his captain this time. He persisted with short-pitched bowling— and the same result. Indulkar hooked at it, and it went flying over backward square leg for six more runs. The Professionals

XI was thus forced to take Akshay off the bowling attack as he was proving to be too costly.

The Amateurs XI had raced to 24 runs off the first over for the loss of no wicket. Indulkar had runs on the board. Akshay had been taught a lesson in humility. Landon's words of encouragement had worked. The crowd's momentum was behind the Amateurs XI now, thanks to the unintelligent bowling that Akshay had just delivered.

Preity could not control the thrill inside her body at this brave hitting from Indulkar. She ran between the seats and jumped across the boundary line, threw her high-heeled shoes away, and ran onto the pitch to congratulate Amay Indulkar.

Stewards ran onto the field to stop Preity from reaching the playing area. But her nimble body was too fast for them to catch. She reached Amay in the middle of the pitch, danced around him, and shook her hips with her shawl on top of her head and sang her favorite Bollywood tunes. The stewards reached her and gently ushered her off the ground. The crowd gave a huge cheer of approval at Preity's innovativeness.

The desired effect on Amay was had. He now had a lovely woman encouraging him to do his best and a mentally strong captain in Landon at the other end of the pitch. He felt his confidence return. There is no better practice than match practice in cricket—something that no amount of net practice sessions can suffice. Indulkar had 24 runs off 6 deliveries faced at an excellent strike rate of 400 percent. He was racing along, and his team needed 120 more runs to win off 19 remaining overs.

Landon did not have to say anything to Amay. He was sure the mere presence of a dancing Preity spurred his young colleague to win them the match.

Udeni Pushpakumara, the Sri Lankan international fast bowler, was next to bowl for the Professionals XI. He had gray-dyed, silvery hair, was thin, tall, and nimble, just as fast and hostile as Akshay.

Landon struck him for a cover drive for four runs and then took a single of the second delivery. Indulkar defended the next three deliveries before setting off for a single off the last to retain the strike. Score: Thirty runs for no loss of wicket. A different bowler was brought in to replace the expensive Akshay. It was the Australian quick bowler from Perth, Dennis Swift.

The match moved along to the sixth over. Landon had moved on to 12 runs. The toll of the captaincy all morning, fielding, the wicket he picked up in the morning, the match fixer's threats on Indulkar's life, and now opening the batting, along with the hectic lifestyle and policing of the last few days caused his body to tire. He had still pushed himself this far, and his team had reached 44 runs, needing 100 more runs to win in the remaining 14 overs, with all 10 wickets intact.

Dennis Swift bowled a good line, and Landon tried to drive but got a leading edge, which Swift caught on his follow-through. Swift then bowled an inswinging yorker to fellow countryman Dean Delaney to rattle his stumps. Delaney was out for zero, and the Professionals XI were back in the game. Score after 6 overs was 44/2.

Enter Ice Cool. He struck two baseball-style sixes over long on but then missed one that turned from a spinner and took the bottom edge of his bat, which went to the wicket-keeper for an easy catch. He was out for 12 and the score after 8 overs was 56/3.

Vivian Rickards came in next to join Indulkar. They put on 26 more runs against the experienced and tight Professionals XI bowling attack and adept fielding. But a direct hit on the stumps from square leg cost Rickards his wicket via a run-out. Rickards out for 20; the score was 82/4 at the end of the twelfth over, with Indulkar batting on 38 runs.

The fourteenth over was leg spin from the Melbourne great Noel Warnes, and he easily claimed the wickets from Inspector Bob Davidson for 6 runs and Ling Zhang-Hue for 1 run, both bowled around their legs with huge spinning leg-breaks.

Score at the end of 14 overs: 97 runs for the loss of 6 wickets for the Amateurs XI. Indulkar was still batting on 46 runs, nearly half his team's score. The opposition captain was not keen to bring back Akshay into the bowling attack because the Amateurs now only needed 47 more runs to win in 36 available deliveries, and with Indulkar still on strike and batting beautifully and anchoring the innings, a similar display like over number 1 could cost them the match.

The match was in fine balance. The spectators were in nervous expectation of a close contest, going all the way down to the wire.

Forty-seven more runs needed, 36 deliveries allowed, 4 wickets in hand, Indulkar still there.

Paddy McNally, the Irish all-rounder, scored runs off the sixteenth over by scoring 4, 2, 2, 6, 6, 0 in the 6 deliveries. By the end of the seventeenth over, the score was 118/7 wickets, with Indulkar on 49 and McNally on 20 runs.

Twenty-six more runs to win off 18 deliveries with 4 wickets in hand.

But the match ebbed and flowed toward both sides, and it was now the loss of McNally's wicket in the first ball of the eighteenth over. Chris Dawson came in to loud applause from the crowd as the son of the chief organizer of the tournament, and Hedwig was courteous enough to stand and wave at his son.

Chris struck a 6 and then a 4 to inch the Amateurs XI even closer to victory. Indulkar took a single that brought up his workman like 50. He received a generous round of applause from the Lord's stadium. At the end of the eighteenth over, they were 129/7.

Fifteen more runs to win off 12 deliveries and 3 wickets in hand, and Indulkar was still batting on 50 runs.

There were no other bowlers left as they had all finished their required maximum quota of overs. Akshay was brought back into the attack for the penultimate and nineteenth over, and he bowled 3 good length deliveries that swung and were left alone by Indulkar. Indulkar took it one ball at a time and watched the remaining 3 deliveries closely and intelligently worked them for 3 successive boundaries. Prcity was delirious with joy in the stands. Indulkar had moved on to 62 runs, his team to 141/7, and the amateurs only needed 3 more runs to win off 6 deliveries remaining in the match, with 3 wickets in hand. Could the amateurs upset the professionals again?

The final over was to be bowled by Dennis Swift. He bowled a yorker and knocked out Chris Dawson's off-stump first ball, and Chris was out for 10 runs, the total 141/8. Ray Shade was bowled first ball for a duck, and the score was 141/9. The match had turned on its head yet again.

Four deliveries left. Three runs to win for the Amateurs XI. One wicket to take for a Professionals XI win. Indulkar was not on strike as the last man Keans came in to bat.

Keans had to take a single to get Indulkar to score the remaining runs. The third ball hit Keans on the pads. Loud shout of leg before wicket from the Professionals XI fieldsmen—Preity had chewed all her manicured nails at this point. Indulkar, at the nonstriker's end, was praying for it to be given not out. Umpire Harold Birds gave it not out. Indulkar, standing next to umpire Birds, felt the temperature of the fielding side drop at those reassuring words from the umpire. "Drifting down leg side."

The next ball from Swift also struck Keans on the bat and pads but, this time, it ballooned to deep fine leg for Akshay to pick up. He saw Indulkar running to the striker's end to score the run (a leg bye), but Akshay, full of rage, had decided, much to his captain's displeasure, to attempt to throw the ball directly to the stumps on the striker's end to run out Indulkar. He was still riled by the brilliant catch Indulkar took that morning to dismiss him. His throw was wide of the stumps, and the wicket-keeper could not reach it despite diving to the ball, and the ball went to the forward mid on boundary, where there was no fielder. Akshay collapsed to the ground in shame. Indulkar easily completed running two more runs with Keans to win the game for the Amateurs XI by one wicket.

Indulkar and Keans, bats waving in the air, ran off the field in jubilation and into the dressing rooms to rapturous applause from the crowds at Lord's.

This photo finish of a razor-sharp final gave the Amateurs XI an unexpected and upset 2-1 series win over their much-fancied international Professionals XI team. This was despite losing the services of their coach after their first game and heavily losing the second game and debuting so many newcomers, including two from countries that do not even play cricket regularly.

The awards ceremony that soon followed had the announcer say, "A team that contained a courageous captain, who also happened to be a law enforcement officer who investigated the murder of the coach, fought off villains, travelled all over the UK and halfway across the world, and also coached his team. He staved off attempts to his life, scored fourteen runs, and took a wicket. A true captain's all-round display, ladies and gentlemen, Landon Beau." The crowd clapped for Landon.

"And the man of the match, who scored sixty-two runs not out, carrying his bat throughout the innings—Amay Indulkar." Rapturous applause from the crowd followed.

His teammates carried him on their shoulders and ran around the ground for a lap of honor. Landon looked a man in a tizzy. He had achieved the impossible and turned defeat into victory.

Hedwig Dawson was all smiles. Orson was dancing around the aisles with his playgirls. Skittle was shouting mechanically over and over, "Three cheers, hip hip hooray!"

The match fixers were furious! Adam, lurking near the sandwich area, growled, "Just wait till I get my hands on that little whippersnapper, Amay!"

As the teammates walked up the stairs, Landon's shirt was tugged by a lady in the crowd. It was Lucy.

The whole stadium wanted a piece of Landon. His lady Amelia wanted him. He really had little time to spare for Lucy. Not when there were dozens of spectators on either side wanting his autograph and picture.

Lucy spoke, her distinctive blue eyes staring into Landon, "Congratulations! I want to tell you that it's okay to love Amelia. You could not have prevented what happened to Sabrina. Love conquers all, love is kind, and love is patient."

Landon replied, "You are such an expert in medieval history and my personal life. You should be working for the tabloids, given your breath of knowledge about me!"

Lucy ignored Landon's words and continued, "Tragically, she passed away from an amniotic fluid embolism. You have my sympathies. I bless your union with Amelia. You two make a good team."

Landon asked, "Thanks for the sympathy. I feel I have come to terms with it now, after returning back to the force. And I am so thankful to you for helping me find the Enchanted Willow. Is there anything I can get you? Can we meet for coffee?"

Lucy said, "Oh no, I have new urgent assignments to go on, thanks for the offer. But—you can get me something. I like orchids, and I like art. Get me the best ones you can find, and meet me tomorrow evening at the London Museum off Euston Road at six p.m., beside exhibit number 56 on tier 3. See you. God bless." And she disappeared into the crowd.

In the dressing room, Mr. Lorgat of the ICC approached Landon. "Congratulations, Mr. Landon Beau. That was a beautiful match you gave us. Here's your special bat back. Have you ever considered playing professionally? You also had to solve the murder case in addition to playing and captaining the team. On behalf of the International Cricket Council, you are not only an ordinary good cricket team captain. You are a very, very good captain."

Chapter 25

Unmasking the Murderer

The next day, all dressed in uniform neatly ironed and pressed, Inspector Harrison, Inspector Davidson, and Landon Beau were in a group of three police cars and an arrest vehicle, making their way to Hedwig Dawson's office.

"Are you sure you know who it is?" asked Harrison.

"Of course I do," said Landon, still feeling his muscles ache from the previous day's cricket match. "The reason for my silence is that too much of information was leaked already in this case. I did not want the murderer to know that we found out two days ago who he is. I wanted to catch them by surprise," reasoned Landon.

Hedwig Dawson's headquarters were at the Canary Wharf area of London. They parked in the underground parking lot and took an elevator to Hedwig's chambers.

Hedwig was in a foul mood, as always. They heard his voice yelling across the room, "Skittle, I want Perez Gonzalez of my Mexico office, not Perez Gonsalves of Goa, to call me about the shipments. Cindy, where is the report on the Johannesburg?"

He saw the officers make their way toward him.

"Well, gentlemen, this is most obtrusive. You can make appointments with my secretary to see me, you know," said Hedwig Dawson.

"Mr. Dawson," said Landon, "we need to talk urgently. It's about the case. I have solved it."

Dawson looked stunned. "But you were just playing for my team only yesterday."

Landon continued, "The evidence is overwhelming. I'm afraid I'll need to ask for your permission to reinvestigate the research lab to investigate all of your employees."

Hedwig bellowed, "Some other time. I have a lot of work."

Landon opened the bag he was carrying and showed Hedwig the Enchanted Willow. Hedwig almost fell off his chair at the sight of it.

Hedwig's eyes opened wide. "Blow me! Is that what I think it is—what my ancestor used two hundred years ago to . . . ?"

"The very same," said Landon. "Anyway, we need to talk in your office." They entered Hedwig's office. They saw Skittle, with its bust opened to form the internal computer console, seated to the right of Hedwig's large chair.

Hedwig sat the inspectors down.

Landon began to explain. "Here is how I see what happened in the case.

"It all began with the murderer wanting to cause financial ruin to your empire. Cricket is now a billion-dollar industry. Thanks to the new 20/20 shortened version, it is an ever bigger money machine.

"You stand to lose 350 million pounds if the Amateurs XI lost the series against the Professionals XI. You would gain a further 50 million pounds if the Professionals XI lost to the Amateurs XI, which is what transpired. This added revenue generated by individual countries' leagues, trying to buy your victorious Amateurs XI players off you.

"Your financial worth being 600 billion dollars in the UK media, this cricket experiment of yours was, indeed, a sizable chunk. You really were serious about this, especially when your brother was 'murdered' and the match fixers appeared and threatened Indulkar. It was no wonder that you approached us as soon as you could and were persistent upon us solving the case as soon as we could and even hired private detectives. I appreciate the urgency.

"Quite a few things struck me about this case as being quite odd. Firstly, how easily information got leaked. The private detectives so easily spilled the beans—confidential information, classified stuff—to Adam the match fixer in Manchester. That shouldn't have happened. This was why I could never arrest him whenever he threatened Indulkar, no matter how credible the video evidence of him being present at the coach's room at the time of his 'murder' was."

"If attempts on my life were not bad enough, why go after innocent Amelia? Why cause a drama to attack her in the privacy of her own home?

"The mysterious death of your late wife in 2004 was another big clue. The discovery of selenium in Graeme's body was another big clue. I think your late wife was poisoned by the same substance—I'll come back to this later.

"This is how I see what happened after the first match at Lord's: The match fixers, seeing the stakes so high in this competition, couldn't resist themselves. Seeing the upset victory of the Amateurs XI in the opening match—and seeing Indulkar's majestic hundred—they had to approach him to alter the outcome of the series. Unofficially, they were to gain 200 to 250 billion dollars in the black market for all the match fixing that could have been done in this series.

"They do threaten cricketers sometimes—just to keep them quiet. But the accusation of death threats and the sudden 'death' of Graeme Dawson made the world think they were the murderers. I can confidently say that the match fixers were innocent all along."

The room gasped in astonishment. Hedwig turned to Skittle. "I hope that you are recording all of this?"

Landon Beau continued, "I did some research of my own. It may surprise you that your brother was actually close to a major scientific breakthrough in suspended animation.

"Simply put, it meant that the body appears dead and inanimate when, in actual fact, it's alive. He even compounded hydrogen sulfide into a capsule, which is what I found in his pocket. There is excellent scientific research from Mark Roth's research group and labs in the USA on this subject. He is able to induce suspended animation in mice for up to a few hours, using hydrogen sulfide, and then get them 'back to life' once it's taken out of their system.

"Hydrogen sulfide has the characteristic odor of rotting eggs. I got that smell when I crushed the tablets found in Graeme's pocket. I got them analyzed, and it was confirmed by our labs.

"Anyway, why did he decide to take those tablets in a hotel room on that fateful day? Why did he want himself to go into suspended animation?

"Simple explanation—he was about to get killed by someone and thought this was the best way to save his life temporarily. He takes a few of his hydrogen sulfide capsules, plays dead, and the attacker thinks he has committed suicide and gives up upon killing him.

"Now, we have no evidence or pictures, but Davidson, my girlfriend—Amelia—and I have encountered an assassin, here in London twice and once again when he followed us to India. He got liquidated in the third encounter when he tried to kill me. We have searched for his remains but found none. All we have are international war-crime most-wanted list records of a hulk called Slocum. He was the assassin.

"Slocum liked to strangulate with his bare hands as his preferred method of killing—it came with him being a former South Island, New Zealand, sheep farmer, I suppose. He might have tried this with Graeme. Graeme must have taken his hydrogen sulfide tablets and dropped to the ground in suspended animation—Slocum saw no fun in the killing, and he left.

"But why kill Graeme? He wouldn't hurt a fly. He was just a science researcher and a cricket coach and ex-club and county cricketer?" asked Hedwig Dawson.

At this point, Cindy Fartington entered the room. She was dressed in her characteristic trousers that stopped an inch above her ankles and wore her cheap ankle-high boots.

"Cindy, how many times have I told you to knock?" bellowed Hedwig Dawson.

Landon continued, "So nice of you to join us, Cindy. Please be seated."

He continued, "Graeme knew what was going on. So do I now. It's to do with cricket's new financial skyrocketing success. It's become the fattest of cash cows in the sports market nowadays. And with that—comes greed.

"You were successful in business. But the murderer could not resist the impulse of one big strike to your finances. Simple: cause the Amateurs XI to lose, and you lose a net 350 million pounds. You think negatively as a result of that, more losses follow in other areas, you lose all you have in a few years."

"The motive—I really don't know. I suggest you discuss that with—*her*."

Landon pointed to Cindy Fartington. "Being a backstabber is easy for me to spot. Been there thousand times before. I literally have eyes at the back of my head now."

Hedwig yelled, "You have the audacity to walk into my office and accuse my executive secretary of this heinous crime? You have no proof."

Landon took out another object from his bag. "She was the owner of this." And he placed the automatic rifle on Hedwig's table. "She scratched my neck out of carnal desire at the prematch dinner party. I've had the scratch patterns on my neck analyzed by a forensic team. It is identical to what we see here on this rifle butt and shooting cartridge. She was at least intelligent enough not to leave us any fingerprints.

"She was in charge of your selenium ores in Uzbekistan. This is where she likely came to know of Slocum, who was involved as an assassin during the Russian-Chechnya war. There is research going on in Russia about type 1 diabetes and islet cells in capsules transplanted from sheep—sheep from Invercargill in the South Island of New Zealand. This was probably how Slocum got recruited into the war as an assassin—someone in the import/export of sheep pancreas might have also been involved in the war and came to know of Slocum's immense abilities to kill.

"I also bet if we exhumed your late wife's body, we'd still find heaps of selenium, just like we did in Graeme's body. No wonder he was so ill in the weeks leading to the match. But we have cured him from that.

"Cindy hired Slocum to kill us. She wanted to eliminate Graeme because he was about to retrieve this magical bat and use it to deliberately win his Amateurs XI team the series in order to thwart her plans to destroy your wealth.

"She was after the magic bat herself—to stop us getting our hands on it.

"The intrusion into Amelia's home by Slocum was because you wanted to throw us off track and make us believe the match fixers were after her laptop because she had images of one of them on it from the cricket match she covered.

"Happily, for me, I was raised in a culture where true love is encouraged, and I have just that with Amelia Kanowski. I know you wanted that one-night stand before the third match because you wanted to kill me. Cindy, you can commit a crime—but justice will catch up with you years after because you always leave evidence behind. Can I ask, Cindy, why you behaved the way you did? Do you not like certain people? I'm sure you must hate me by now."

A shaken Cindy gave out a peal of thunderous yelling. "Hedwig, you wanker! I loved you all these years. I worshipped you. You instead married that stripper and whore after meeting her at your friend's bachelor party! I killed her. I loved you. You then got yourself a female robot."

Like an enraged beast, full of hate, Cindy lunged forward to pounce upon and attack Hedwig Dawson—but the inspectors caught her in time.

They arrested Cindy Fartington on counts of attempted murder and conspiring to kill and led her away from the office.

Chapter 26

The Orchids for Lucy

Landon was drained from the morning's events. Cindy Fartington's home at Ealing was scoured for evidence by the New Scotland Yard, and there were plans on selenium poisoning and money transactions to Slocum discovered on her computer files. She confessed to all charges laid by Landon and was awaiting a triple life sentence imprisonment at the magistrate's court in a months' time.

"She's safely in jail, Landon. Thank you for solving the case. Do you still wish to leave the force?" asked Inspector Harrison.

"No, sir," replied Landon. "Solving the crime was only 1 percent of the challenge. The cricket was the other 1 percent. Rather, 98 percent was what else happened during this unexpected adventure."

"What a pity you persist in being so logical, Landon," said Harrison.

"Meet me at my place for a drink tonight, Landon," asked Davidson. "I think some caviar and Dom Pérignon 2005 would be ideal. Bring Amelia along, if she's not working."

"I'll have to take a rain check, sir. I have to meet someone special at the museum tonight," replied Landon.

It was six p.m. Landon wore his finest pinstripe suit. He was standing with a bouquet of multicolored orchids in the London museum, in an empty room beside exhibit number 56 on tier 3, waiting for Lucy to turn up.

She's late, he thought as the time raced to quarter past six. He decided to admire the painting. It was of a beautiful woman with large blue eyes and long, flowing black hair, dressed in a purple corset and flowing evening gown and was dated 1808.

He then caught a smell of Pavlova perfume.

The woman's painting was the only exhibit in the large room. Landon was alone. He heard the sound of high-heeled shoes. He thought that someone was approaching him. Maybe the curator to tell him that it was closing time.

Instead, it was Amelia. "How did she know I was here?" thought Landon.

Amelia approached Landon. She was dressed in a pink miniskirt, and her hair was left loose. She had matching pink lipstick and pink high-heeled shoes and gave Landon an astonished look. "What are you doing here, Landon? And by the way, congratulations on solving the murder case. I heard about it from Bob."

Landon looked at this Prussian beauty who had made his case solving all the more possible. He replied, "Lucy told me to meet her here, after the match, with these flowers."

Amelia was astonished at this and replied, "Lucy also told me to meet her here, dressed in this outfit. But . . . why?"

Landon replied, "It's getting late already. I know of a good Italian place around the corner that can just make ravioli and strawberry dessert."

Amelia accepted the orchids from Landon, and the happy couple left hand in hand.

The lovers were so preoccupied with each other that they failed to notice the painting in detail. The inscription below the painting read, "DAME ANDALUSIA, 1787-1810, DEFENDER OF THE NAME OF CRICKET, ALSO HONORED AS MOTHER CRICKET."

Chapter 27

Adam Catches Up with Indulkar

An excited Preity Lahoria was jumping up and down, barely able to control her excitement. Her father had arranged to meet her hero, Amay Indulkar, to discuss engagement plans.

She wore her favorite red *sari,* dyed her hands with *mehendi*, wore her favorite bangles and earrings and *bindi* and ankle rings, and awaited Amay's arrival. She made sure there were enough savories in the kitchen for their visitor.

She felt like a real woman in an Indian summer at London. She played her favorite Bollywood movie songs loudly, much to her mother's disapproval. Meeting and getting engaged to Amay felt to her as if the very purpose of her existence on earth was about to be fulfilled.

A Mercedes Benz limousine arrived outside Amay's home. All East London wondered what a luxury limousine was doing in their backyard—a lost driver, perhaps, in the wrong part of town? Amay was dressed in the only suit he owned. The driver got out and opened the backseat door for Amay. Amay, not used to such luxury treatment, politely declined. The driver said that he was working for Preity's father and that he was here to take him to their home.

Amay got into the backseat. The chauffer slammed the door shut. He was horrified at whom he saw. Behind the dark glasses was the unmistakable face of the match fixer, Adam, French beard, dark glasses, and all. He had two of his hefty henchmen sitting beside him.

"Don't try to be a hero," said Adam coldly. "There is no mobile phone reception through this limousine, the doors are locked, and it's soundproof. You are now in my power."

Amay tried to struggle, but the henchmen grabbed him and pinned him down to the opposite seat.

"But Preity's dad sent this limousine," he pleaded.

"Amayyyy," replied Adam pensively, "we have people everywhere. Half of Mr. Kishore Lahoria's butlers are paid by us for information. We tapped all of his phones. We heard Mr. Lahoria saying he would send his car to pick you up. Well, we got to you first. Driver must still be on his way, navigating through East London."

Adam grinned. "Anyway, good news for you, boy." Amay's ears picked up those welcome words.

Adam continued, "You see, Amay, you may have heard in the news today that the real murderer of your coach Graeme Dawson was caught. His female secretary did it. We were after you to influence you because billions of dollars in the subcontinent and Middle East were at stake if you got out for zero runs."

Adam continued, "We are not barbarians. We kill people who go to the police and tell them about us. But we are not killers of innocent people. I know how it feels growing up in India. Too many people, too few jobs. I know what it's like to live in poverty like you did. No food to eat. Depressed elders who lived like you when they were young, shouting negative thoughts to make you as negative as they were. The British medical system is totally oblivious to how many doctors they bring into this country and then abruptly throw all of you good Indian doctors out. So much of job insecurity. I admire the way you have come up in life. The way you have adapted to Britain. *Shabaash* [well done].

"But, Amay, we have to do our job. And the world wrongly thought all these days that we killed Graeme. You have to really be very thankful to your cricket captain Landon for solving the case.

"Landon listened to me. I am a sinner, a money lover, but Landon listened to me. He knew I was innocent. He knew I did not kill Graeme. Why should I kill Graeme?

"Landon caught the real murderess. It was Cindy Fartington. We were relieved. My bosses back in the subcontinent are relieved that the real blame is given to the real culprit. So now, we're even.

"So we have decided to forgive you for not doing what we told you to do and scoring those sixty-two runs at Lord's. In any case, you did not receive any money from us. But if you play in another match, we will approach you again."

Indulkar listened to those words. "Adam," he said, "I play cricket just for pleasure. I am going to retire now and pursue medicine. I have just been offered a nice two-year medical senior house officer job at the Wigan Infirmary. I don't need to play cricket again. I'll get engaged to Preity Lahoria. What you do with other cricketers is your business." He said those words as the car stopped outside Mr. Lahoria's mansion in Earl's Green.

As Indulkar got out of the car, he heard Adam's last few words in Urdu. "God bless you, young man. You are my inspiration." The limousine sped away into the London night.

Graeme Dawson spontaneously recovered from the suspended animation that afternoon. He had induced himself on the night of his attempted murder by swallowing his own hydrogen sulfide capsules to avoid being killed in a gruesome way by Slocum. He gave his testimony to the police, and they hailed the accuracy between his version of events and Landon Beau's version.

Chapter 28

Double Engagement Party

It took place on the fifteenth of August 2010. It was a joint ceremony that took place at the Leeds. Landon and Amay were dressed in the finest formal suits. Preity was dressed in a traditional red *sari*—with lots of bangles, a large *bindi*, fresh flowers pinned to her hair, and elaborate *mehendi* all over her hands, arms, and feet. Amelia was dressed in a one-piece golden yellow frock, with folded ends as it tapered toward her feet, with a sleeveless top, a golden necklace of the Sydney Opera house, and her hair left loose, with gold lipstick and blue mascara.

After the engagement ceremony, a large party took place later that evening at Harewood House in Leeds, one of the best and most popular wedding reception venues in all West Yorkshire. The entire Amateurs XI team was there as guests, with their extended family and friends. Landon sang the song *"(Everything I Do) I Do It for You"* by Bryan Adams to Amelia Kanowski, while Paddy McNally sang "I Will Always Love You" by Whitney Houston to Preity on Amay Indulkar's behalf. The food included Indian *masala dosas* and *paneer* as openers, the various biryanis and myriads of curried meats, along with tapas, salmon, lamb rumps, and baked vegetables—that constituted the main course—followed, and the *rasgullas* and *gulab jamuns*, black forest cakes, lava cakes, and cheesecakes were served as dessert.

Hedwig Dawson was hopelessly drunk. Adam the match fixer was spotted dancing with the android Skittle, who had a new dress for the engagement party. The couples kissed and embraced to the tune of rock band Bon Jovi playing "It's My Life." A recovered and rehabilitated Graeme Dawson, in a wheelchair, admired the difference Landon had made to cricket.

Dame Andalusia's spirit smiled in heaven at the sweetness cricket had brought to these people. Sunshine and happiness prevailed. Love drove Landon to all his victories, in cracking the crime case and in winning the cricket match. Love, Landon realized, is the strongest motivator in winning life's challenges. Love and cricket were the overall winners as they had, yet again, conquered all.